The Case of the Waltzing Mouse

The Case of
The Waltzing Mouse

A
BRAINS
BENTON
MYSTERY

by GEORGE WYATT

Illustrated by AL SCHMIDT

GOLDEN PRESS 🕊 NEW YORK

Contents

Chapter 1

Of Mice and Money

"EEEEEEEEEEEK! . . . EEEEEEEEEEEK! . . . EEEEK! . . . EEEEK! . . . EEEEK!"

The blood-curdling sounds screeched against the ceiling, bounced off the walls, and set off echoes weird enough to send jet streams of fear rocketing up and down the spines of brave men.

"Was ist das? Was ist das?" The guttural shout intermingled with the screams.

I looked across the room at my partner and shrugged my shoulders. He looked back at me with hands outstretched, palms up in a "So-what-did-you-expect?" gesture.

Monkeys were chattering. Birds whistling. Mice hopping about. A seal was applauding with his flippers. He seemed to be enjoying the pandemonium as much as my partner and I were.

Now I guess I'd better put you in the picture. (That's a phrase I've often heard Police Officer McKeon use.) The screaming and shouting and chattering were taking place in the small auditorium of the Crestwood Garden Club. It was all started by one innocent little white mouse.

All this mouse did was jump from a table to my sister Ann's shoulder.

She screamed.

My mother ran over to see what was the matter with Ann. The mouse jumped from Ann's shoulder to my mother's.

She screamed.

The professor shouted.

The monkeys chattered.

The birds whistled.

The seal applauded.

Creeps! What a scene! What a riot! What a laugh!

Maybe I'd better go back to the beginning and tell you what a rodent was doing at a garden club, and as an invited guest, at that. And maybe I'd better tell you who I am. I'm Jimmy Carson. I live in Crestwood at 43 Maple Street. I'm a detective. I'm one half of the Benton and Carson International Detective Agency. I'm the secretary-treasurer of the firm and its chief cook and bottle washer. By that I mean I always get all the dirty jobs.

My partner and president of the firm is Barclay "Brains" Benton. He's the thinker of the firm, as I suppose you would deduce from his nickname.

Even though we're both still in junior high, and most adults, I guess, would call us kids, we've been in on some real thrillers, some real mysteries. And we've solved them, too. All you have to do is look us up in the back issues of the *Crestwood Daily Ledger* and read about the cases we've cracked.

But to get back to the auditorium. All those animals were part of a show. This show had been put on for the benefit of the Crestwood Community Camp Fund. This is a local organization that raises money to send poor to a summer camp on Lake Carmine for a couple of weeks. My mother was very keen on the whole idea. She's a great club-woman. She'd helped raise the money to get the camp started. Brains and I had been in on it, too. The money my mother and others raised had been stolen. Brains and I got it back. That's one of the cases the *Ledger* wrote up. You may have seen it— we called it the *Case of the Stolen Dummy*.

The animal show belonged to a man named Professor Gustave Von Maltzbenden. He traveled around in a combination trailer-zoo, playing the charity bazaar circuit. He'd keep half the proceeds and the other half would go to a charity or to a worthwhile cause like our Community Camp Fund.

When Brains and I arrived at the clubhouse that morning we saw the professor's trailer-zoo. In big letters on each side there was a sign:

GUSTAVE THE GREAT'S
AMAZING AGGREGATION
OF
ARTISTIC ANIMALS
IN
TALENTED TRICKS & TURNS OF TERPSICHORE

Brains and I had stood there looking at it. Boy, it was really impressive. I had turned to Brains.

"Looks like we're going to see some show," I said. "But what's that word mean—that last one, 'terp-see-chore'?"

"The word, my uninformed friend," Brains replied, and I didn't miss that note of sarcasm in his voice, "comes from Greek mythology. It is the name of the Muse of dancing and choral song. And, for your further enlightenment, you have fallen into a common error and mispronounced the word. The correct pronunciation is 'turp-*sick*-or-ree.' "

See what I mean? No wonder he's called "Brains." But don't get me wrong—and make real sure you don't get *him* wrong. He may be skinny and wear glasses and talk like a walking encyclopedia, but he's wiry, hasn't an ounce of fear on his lanky body, and he's also the best pitcher our junior high ever had. What a fast ball he's got!

There must have been about a hundred excited kids and their mothers at the Garden Club auditorium that morning. They had seen a mouse do a dance, a slow, graceful waltz. His name was Xenophon, and he's the little rascal who started all the racket by jumping on my sister's shoulder. Then Oscar, the musical seal had played "America" on a set of horns. Real good too, except he hit the wrong horn now and again and the song came out kind of flat.

Two monkeys called Bing and Bang had done an act on a trapeze. The birds, parakeets, love birds and canaries, had given a song recital, very seriously conducted by the Herr Professor. Then there was a snake, too. All it did was lie coiled up, sleeping. But it sort of gave me the shudders to look at it.

All in all, it had been a good show. It lasted about an hour and a half. It wowed the little kids. I have to admit that even Brains and I had chuckled plenty at the acts. When it was over, and the small fry and their mothers had filed out, Ann, Brains and I waited until my mother settled up accounts with Professor Gustave. Then he asked if we'd help him load his animals back into the trailer.

"Ach! I am so glad if you can do this by me. Until just one, two—no, three days ago I have helper. Young man —I call him 'Blackie.' His name is Harry."

I looked at Brains. His eyebrows had shot up at this remark, too. The professor called his former helper "Blackie" because his name was Harry.

Does that make sense?

But the professor had gone right on talking.

"His name is Harry Blackstone. So, for the short, vee call him 'Blackie.' You understood?"

Vee understood. The professor's German accent was pretty strong. All his w's came out v's.

"Blackie, he is with me for two years—since he is only just out of the high school. For a while, he is goot boy, but he becomes bad boy ven he becomes man. He does not like my animals. Always he is teasing my little Xenophon. Finally, I tell him, 'Go! Out! Raus!' "

The Herr Professor had the mouse in his big red hands at this point. He brought it up and let it nibble at his cheek, caressing it with his other hand.

"Now who could help but love (he pronounced the word 'luff') my little Xenophon?"

My mother and Ann were standing about five feet away. From the expressions on their faces, I could have mentioned to Professor Gus two people who would have no trouble at all not "luffing" Xenophon.

"And then, Blackie he becomes mean to Oscar," Professor Gus continued.

Oscar was the seal. At the mention of his name, the seal reared up and started smacking his flippers together.

"Oh, vell, my troubles you do not vant to listen at. So, now by the trailer vee put the animals. Nein?"

He meant "yes," but he said "nein," which means "no." I was beginning to feel that if I had to listen to the professor much more, I wouldn't know whether I was upside down or downside up.

It was just after this that almost everything in the auditorium suddenly turned downside up—uh, I mean upside down.

The professor had walked over to the platform where Oscar the seal was lying, taking everything in, and giving out with a bark now and then. He was hungry, and when Oscar was hungry, he barked—just like a dog, only deeper, something like the combination of a dog's bark and a frog's croak.

Professor Gus opened the lid of the wicker fishing creel he wore slung around his neck, took out a couple of fish and tossed them to Oscar. Then he unslung the creel and put it on a chair.

"First, vee taking out the birds," he said. He came walking back to the bird cages. As he passed my mother and Ann, he put Xenophon down on a table near where they were standing.

That's when it started. That's when Xenophon leaped onto my sister's shoulder and that's when those female sirens went off. I expect you could hear them in Middlebury, forty miles away. That's more than you can say for Crestwood fire whistles.

The firm of Benton and Carson went into action. I jumped for Xenophon and Xenophon jumped for Brains. Mother collapsed onto a chair, and Ann threw her arms around the professor for protection. Brains deftly caught Xenophon, and reached out to hand him to the professor. Ann saw Xenophon being poked back toward her and let out another shriek.

The professor took the mouse and clucked to him.

"Here's a nice piece of Limburger cheese, mine friend," he said, popping something in Xenophon's mouth.

Then he put him in the pocket of his coat and things began to calm down. Mother and Ann became quiet. Then the animals, figuring the show was really over now, calmed down, too.

All but Oscar the seal. Oscar raised the front part of his torso and began applauding. Maybe he wanted an encore. He didn't get it, though. As he was flapping his flippers, one of them struck the fish-creel. It banged to the floor, and a little door in the bottom popped open.

Out of that door spilled money. More money than I'd ever seen or ever expect to see. Bundles of bright-green one-, five-, ten- and twenty-dollar bills.

My eyes bugged out. Brains' red hair seemed to stand on end.

What was the owner of a traveling animal show doing carrying all that money?

I guess Brains must have scented a mystery right off. His face lighted up. Mine fell. I had been thinking only of the vacation we were to start on that day—two weeks at Lake Carmine. Two weeks of fishing, water skiing and swimming. And NO detecting. I couldn't have been more wrong!

Chapter 2

Lakeward Bound

Now don't get me wrong. I like detecting. If I didn't, I'd have given it up long ago. It can be plenty exciting, but it can also be plenty dangerous and scary. Believe me, being a detective can get you into plenty of jams, and I don't mean the kind made out of strawberries.

But Brains and I had just wound up one of the most dangerous cases in the history of our detective firm, and I felt we both deserved a good long rest, a real vacation. Oh, we'd be back on the job sooner or later. Both of us like to solve mysteries and see that justice is done. So, if you've got any private-eye jobs, remember the name of our firm: Benton and Carson.

We do all sorts of sleuthing—shadowing, tracing of missing persons, we're on the job twenty-four hours a day, and we're quite agreeable to free consultation.

Right now, though, the firm was very busy rounding up birds, monkeys, mice, seals and money. Oh yes, the professor had one other performer in his aggregation—a talking crow, named of all things, Edgar Allan Crow.

"Very clever play on words," Brains had said when he heard the name. "But Edgar Allan Poe wrote about a raven."

Funny part of it was, old E. A. Crow hadn't peeped during all the ruckus. He'd hopped into his cage without any fuss, too.

Once we had the professor's pets set, things quieted down. Brains, who had put himself in charge of the money, was crouched down, squatting on his haunches, his arms upraised and holding out two bundles of money he had picked up. Did he ever look funny! I could only think of one thing. With his bony knees bent and his long arms stretched out, he looked exactly like a praying mantis.

His eyes, though, were still on that money. I could imagine what his mind was on. If there was the remotest possibility of any mystery, Brains wanted to be in on it.

Brains looked up at the professor.

"It is quite obvious, sir," he said, "that you have little or no faith in the banking institutions of America."

Herr Professor Gus only looked puzzled.

"I mean, Professor, don't you think it would be safer to have such a sum of money as this reposing in a guarded bank vault, safely insured by the Federal Deposit Insurance Corporation?"

"Ach, now it is the light I am seeing. You are asking me vy I carry such a sum of money instead of into the bank putting it?"

"That is correct, sir."

"You see, young man, I am on the road always, traveling from one town to another. From here, my next show I am giving in Mittleberg."

"Mittleberg?" I cut in.

"I believe, Jimmy, the professor means Middlebury."

"Dot's right. So, since I am never in one town more than one, two, maybe three days, banks I can not use. Anyvay, who would ever bother to steal from old man like me?"

Well, the professor sure had more confidence in human nature than most people have, especially when it comes to money. There wasn't any way of telling, but he must have had seven or eight thousand dollars stowed away in that creel. The money was in a false metal bottom attached to the creel. Looking at the creel, you'd think it was like any other one that a fisherman might use. The professor, of course, used it to carry Oscar's food in—the top part, I mean.

I just hoped nobody ever would try to steal from a nice old gentleman like the professor. I don't know exactly how old he was, maybe in his late fifties or early sixties. His hair was pure white, and he had plenty of it. When he hopped around, as he did when he was leading Xenophon's waltz, his hair flew around and stuck up as if it were being pulled by an electric magnet. Maybe you've seen pictures of that famous scientist, Albert Einstein. That's the kind of hair the professor had.

We got the animals loaded into the trailer-zoo. It was fixed up fine for the animals. There were cages for the birds and the monkeys and the snake. And in the rear of the trailer there was a tank with water in it. That was for Oscar, of course. By the time we'd finished loading the trailer, I envied Oscar. I'd have crawled right in the tank with him, I was that hot. Visions of a long cool dive in Lake Carmine danced in my head. I could hardly wait to get going.

We waved good-by to the professor, and he turned his trailer-zoo in the direction of the highway leading to Mittleberg—sorry, I mean Middlebury. My mother and I got into our car, and Brains and Ann followed us in Ann's jalopy.

We drove to my house first and had a quick snack. I was anxious to get on the road. You see, Brains and I were going on ahead of my parents to open up the cottage. My dad had rented the cottage for two weeks.

Some years we'd rent it for the first half of July and the Bentons, they're Brains' parents, would take it for the second half. That way Brains and I had a whole month on the lake.

This year, though, the Bentons were too busy at Crestwood College to take a vacation. Brains' father was a professor of history at the school, and Mrs. Benton taught art there. So, with only two weeks at the lake this year, I wanted to make the most of them.

We loaded some of our things in Ann's jalopy. Mom insisted on kissing me good-by. Gosh, you'd think I was off on a 'round-the-world trip and wouldn't be back for months. Actually she and Dad were coming out to the lake that same afternoon, just as soon as he got off work.

Ann had a job that summer at the Community Camp as a swimming instructor. She had been given the day off to help at the benefit show. That's why Brains and I were able to go on out to our cottage ahead of my parents. Ann was going to drop us off on her way back to camp.

From my house, we went next to Brains'. The old jalopy was purring just as pretty as a cat full of cream. Ann had bought the old heap early in the spring. Brains and I had worked on it, and if I do say so, we had done a mighty fine job—with a little help from the Acme Garage.

Brains lives only a few blocks from my house, on Chestnut Drive. The house is a big old rambling white frame structure. But the best part of the house is what's in back of it—Brains' crime laboratory. This had been a carriage house in the horse and buggy days. Now, the second floor had been turned over to Brains by his parents, and no one, believe me, NO one was allowed in it except me and even I had to give the password. Once in a while, we let in some other boy who might be helping us on a case, but never, never, was an adult permitted to enter.

Ann braked to a stop in front of Brains' house.

"Hurry up, Brains," my sister said. "I want to get back to camp in time for my four o'clock swimming class."

Brains looked at his watch. "It is just after two, now," he said. "I was hoping you might be able to spare me five minutes while I check on an experiment I am conducting in the crime lab."

Ann gave a grunt of annoyance, tightened her lips and stared crossly at Brains.

"All right," she said finally. "Five minutes. Not one second longer. I know you. When you get your nose stuck in an experiment, time means nothing."

Brains shot me a quick look. I knew what he meant. As a sister, Ann is all right. But after all, she is a girl, and girls and women just don't understand how it is when a fellow gets interested in something highly scientific and technical.

"Honest, Ann. I won't take long. I received a piece of equipment yesterday and began a twenty-four-hour test run on it. I merely want to check it out and shut off the power."

"Well, hur-ry," she replied sternly.

I scooted along after Brains, ignoring my sister's call of "Jimmy, you don't have to go along too, do you?"

We slipped through the secret panel on one side of the carriage house—we call it a garage—and mounted the folding stairs that came snaking down when Brains pushed a hidden button. Then we were inside the crime lab.

If you can imagine a sort of combination research laboratory, machine shop and the inside of one of those block houses where they control the firing of rockets, then you'll get some idea of what the crime lab looked like. Everywhere you'd look, you'd see microscopes, test tubes, power tools, electronic gear and bottles filled with all kinds of liquids.

There wasn't much Brains didn't have in the crime lab, and he kept adding to it every month.

Right now he was examining something that looked to me like a vacuum cleaner. It had a long wire coming out of one end with a round metal disc on it, and a pair of earphones was attached to the other end.

"What's this thing?" I asked Brains.

Brains didn't answer at once. He was fiddling with some dials on the side of the thing. I leaned over his red head and saw the hand on an indicator waver back and forth between − 5 and 0 and + 5. When the needle came to a rest on 0, Brains shut off a switch. There was a big smile on his face.

"It works," he said. "If I only had a few more hours, I could check it out further, make some minute, final adjustments, then it would be ready for an operational test."

"Thanks a lot," I replied. Brains had a way of ignoring direct questions—my direct questions—at times that got under my skin.

"So, I repeat: what is that thing?"

"It is a device I have been working on for the past ten days. I had hoped it would be perfected in time to take it with us to Lake Carmine. But, it still needs a few more hours of laboratory testing. So, since your sister Ann is so anxious to be on the way, I fear I will have to leave it here."

You see what I mean? He still hadn't told me what the thing was. I was about to erupt like Vesuvius when Ann's honking the horn on the jalopy put out my volcano.

We left the lab. I still didn't know what Brains had been inventing. And, of course, I had no way of knowing then that within a few days, this "device" was going to figure big in a new mystery we were unknowingly heading for.

I didn't know either, at that time, that for a part of our vacation, the firm of Benton and Carson were going to be baby sitters for a waltzing mouse and a musical seal.

That's the sort of thing, though, that detectives can always run into—you just never know what's going to pop up next.

A few minutes and a few hundred words from Ann later (because we had overstayed our allotted five minutes in the lab) we turned left from Tinker Drive onto Washington Avenue and headed north to the Middlebury Highway.

Once the outskirts of Crestwood were behind us, Ann stepped down a little harder on the gas pedal and we were on our way. We didn't go too fast. Ann's a careful driver for a girl. The jalopy putt-putted right along. Now and then it gave out with a protesting snort, and Ann would give us a worried look. But we just ignored her. What do girls know about cars, anyway?

For the first few miles, we just chattered away about a lot of things, Ann doing most of the chattering, telling us a million things we ought to have done by the time Mom and Dad got to the cottage. Then, right out of nowhere, Brains asked this puzzler:

"What would happen to all those animals if anything should befall the professor?"

"Befall the professor? You mean if anything should happen to him?" I asked.

"That is precisely what I mean."

"But what could happen to him?" Ann asked. "He's such a nice, harmless old gentleman."

"Are you forgetting all the money he has with him?" Brains asked in reply.

"Creeps! That's right," I said. "He's traveling all alone."

"Of course, the money is cleverly concealed," Brains added. "Still, it is likely that there must be others than ourselves who know of its whereabouts."

We were quiet for a few minutes. We'd come about twenty miles on the highway. Our turn-off onto Lake Shore Road North was only a few miles away. This is the road that runs all the way around the lake. Lake Carmine lies east-and-west. It's about twenty miles long and about ten miles wide at its widest point. The cottage we had that summer was on Lake Shore Road North, about ten miles east of the Middlebury Highway, on the other side of Knob Point.

The camp where Ann was a counselor this summer is on the southern side of the lake, diagonally across the lake and a couple of miles to the west of where our cottage is located.

"Well, it's a good thing the professor and his zoo and his money aren't going to be around Crestwood any longer," Ann said, coming back to the subject. "Because I know you two—you'd want to make a big mystery out of it, and you'd be in big trouble again."

Big trouble, she said. Now isn't that just like a sister? We'd been in situations that gave us a lot of trouble solving, but aside from a few close calls, a couple of scary chases, and some real mean people trying to stop us by any means they could find, we'd never been in big trouble. Women! Always exaggerating!

Neither Brains nor I replied to Ann's crack about us and the mysteries we had solved. I learned long ago not to argue with a sister—especially, I guess, when she's older than you are and thinks she knows so much more.

Anyway, we had reached Lake Shore Road North, and Ann turned off. Just to the right, between the road and the lake, there's a small amusement park. It's called Wonder Park. It has a merry-go-round, a Ferris wheel, a Tunnel of Thrills. It has a very nice beach, too, with boats and canoes for hire, and even a speedboat you can rent if you want to go water skiing.

"We've got to come over here for some water skiing," I said to Brains. "That kicker on the boat that goes with the cottage isn't powerful enough for skiing." I was referring to the twelve-foot dinghy and its ten-horse outboard that came with the rental of the cottage.

Wonder Park is only open afternoons and evenings, except on Saturday. It gets most of its customers from Middlebury, although there's always a good sprinkling of Crestwood people to be found there. It's really a very well run park. Lots of families go there for a day of picnicking and fun.

We had gone about a mile beyond the park when Brains suddenly sat up.

"Stop!" he called out. He craned his neck forward. "Stop the car!"

Ann did and Brains leaped out. I was right behind him. I had spotted the same thing that caused Brains to ask Ann to stop.

It was Professor Gustave's trailer-zoo. What in the world, I wondered, hot-footing it after Brains, was it doing here? The professor was supposed to be on his way to Middlebury.

We raced up to the trailer. The animals were setting up a terrific uproar, worse than the one they'd put on back in Crestwood.

They had been abandoned. They were frantic with fear.

Chapter 3

Footprints in the Sand

"Oh, you poor things!"

Those were the first words spoken. And by my sister Ann, at that. She was going from one side of the trailer to the other, trying to calm down the animals. Only a couple of hours before, she'd been screaming because a tiny little old mouse jumped on her shoulder. Now she was all sympathy. How can you figure it?

"We've got to find the professor," Brains said. I could hardly hear him: the monkeys were chattering like mad, Oscar the seal was barking his head off, and Edgar Allan Crow was letting out one indignant "Caw-caw," after another.

The trailer-zoo was parked about halfway between the lake's edge and the road. While Ann was trying to get the animals to settle down, Brains and I started searching for the professor.

"I don't think he can be far away," Brains said. "He's only been here half an hour or so."

"How do you figure that?" I asked. "He could have been here over an hour. He left Crestwood long before we did."

We had reached the edge of the lake when I asked my question.

"Your powers of observation, my friend," Brains said, "must not be too acute today. Remember, even on a vacation, a detective should always be on the alert."

"Some vacation so far," I mumbled back. Brains didn't pay any attention to me. He went right on talking.

"Perhaps you didn't notice that wax paper over there?" He pointed to a spot about ten feet back from the lake shore.

"Sure. Someone had a picnic here, so what?"

Brains walked over and picked up the wax paper.

"Try this nearer your nostrils. I detected the odor as we walked past it."

Brains pushed the wax paper under my nose, and I leaped back as if he were pushing a rattlesnake in my face. What a smell! Smell is really a polite word for the odor coming from that piece of wax paper.

"Limburger." That was Brains' one word comment.

Ever smelled Limburger cheese? Don't. That was my first whiff of it, and I hope my last one.

"What did the professor give his mouse to calm him after the excitement in the auditorium?" Brains asked.

"Hey, that's right," I exclaimed, "he gave him Limburger cheese. Do you think the professor goes for it, as well as Xenophon?"

"It's a popular cheese in Germany," he replied. "And Professor Von Maltzbenden is certainly German."

I couldn't argue with that.

"But what's all that got to do with the professor's not being here more than an hour?" I demanded of Brains.

"Before coming down here, I felt the radiator of the car used by the professor to pull the trailer. It was still quite warm to my touch. Also, although your sister Ann is a very careful driver, I'm sure she goes faster than the professor does."

From what Brains was saying I knew he was off on one of his deduction kicks, like Sherlock Holmes. Brains rather fancies himself as a junior-size Sherlock, and with that long nose of his, he looks something like Holmes.

"So, if it took us forty-five minutes to get here, and it did, then I'm certain it took the professor a good hour and a half. He left Crestwood two hours ago. He spent fifteen minutes, let us say, eating his sandwich. Then he disappeared."

He had disappeared, all right. That much even I could deduce. I'm not as strong on this deduction stuff as Brains is, but anyone can tell when someone isn't around.

We kept on searching. Brains was walking along the edge of the beach, his head bent down, his shoulders humped over, and his eyes focussed on the sand.

I went over to him.

"Footprints. Recently made," Brains said.

I got down on my hands and knees and examined the footprints.

"How can you tell they've been recently made?"

"You will notice," Brains replied, "that at the deepest part of the depression made by the foot, the sand is still slightly damp. It has not been exposed to the sun long enough for it to have become completely dry. We will follow these prints."

We did, but it wasn't easy. From the path made by the footprints, it looked as if whoever made them was staggering. We tracked them for maybe fifty, seventy-five feet, when they suddenly veered off to the left, leading into a small stand of woods. Our trail came to an end. It would have taken Daniel Boone himself to follow those footprints on the hard ground, strewn with leaves and pine needles.

Brains tried for a while. Then, with a disappointed look on his face, he finally gave up. We made our way back to the spot where Brains' long nose had sniffed out the Limburger.

"Well, what do we do next?" I asked.

"We must ponder the situation. We must put ourselves in the position of the professor, Operative Three."

Operative Three he was calling me! Right then, I knew Brains was lost in being a detective again. You see, Operative Three is my code name. Brains is Operative X. Don't ask me what ever happened to Operatives One and Two, because there just never were any. But the thing is, we never use our code names unless we're working on a case.

I guess Brains must have automatically figured we were on a case when we found the abandoned trailer-zoo with the professor missing.

While Brains was doing his pondering, I wandered a few feet down the beach in the other direction. And *I* made a discovery.

"Brains!" I shouted. "Come here."

Brains came on the double, his long skinny legs scissoring up the space.

"How about this for a discovery," I said, kind of proud of myself. "Look how the sand is all mussed up right here. No clear prints. Then if you will notice, Operative X"—jeepers, I was back in business, too—"if you'll notice, two sets of pretty plain footprints lead back up the bank toward the road. And from the distance between the prints, I'd say they were made by someone in an awful hurry."

"Quite right, Operative Three. Those footprints were obviously made by two men running."

"Then wouldn't you say that a fight, or some kind of struggle took place here? And then the fighters took off?"

"My congratulations to you, Operative Three. Your powers of observation have returned to you, somewhat. Mentally, let us reconstruct what could have taken place."

Brains stood for a moment stroking his chin.

"If my theory is correct," he reasoned, "I would assume that two men attacked the professor. Something frightened them off during the attack. That double set of prints must have been made by the attackers fleeing. I am puzzled, however. Why does the first set of footprints we found start a good twenty feet down the beach—away from the scene of the struggle?"

Brains stalked around for a while bent over like a bloodhound. I just stood watching him.

"Operative Three," he suddenly barked at me. "Come here." Brains pointed at the exact spot where the jumbled-up sand showed signs of a fight. "Stand here."

I did just what he said without comment, but I was thinking, "Now what?"

"You," said Brains, "are the professor. You are an elderly man; your mind is foggy, because two men have just attacked you. But you have one clear thought in mind—your animals." Brains fixed me with his eyes like a phony hypnotist. "You must get to them," he added in a deep voice.

Now, I'm no movie star, but if I do say so myself, I put out a good performance. I rubbed my head, shook it and waddled off up the path toward the trailer. I was just really getting into the part when Brains called, "Your head is whirling. You are lost, confused. Return this way."

I swung around and staggered back toward the lake, still acting. I closed my eyes to make it good and realistic. Suddenly, I felt my feet dig into the sand. I had zigzagged off the path, out of the woods and down onto the beach.

"That's it. Absolutely!" I heard Brains shout. He came running up to me.

"See, when you stagger up toward the trailer, you are on hard ground. No footprints. As you lose direction, you end up on the beach, right where I found the first trail of prints. So— just so—did the professor. That's why his prints are so far from the scene of the fight."

"Jeepers, I'll bet you're right on the nose," I said proudly. As usual, Brains paid me no attention.

"I only wish I had some plaster," he muttered.

I didn't have to ask why, I knew he'd go right on and tell me whether I asked or not. He did.

"If I could make a mold of one of these footprints, then I might be able to tell what type of boot made the print."

"What do you mean 'boot'?"

"I mean 'shoe,' of course. But Europeans call their footwear 'boots.' You must understand, Operative Three, that we can't be positive that these footprints were made by the professor. We can assume they were. But, if I had a mold of the footprint, I could tell whether the maker of these prints wore American or European shoes."

And I'll bet you a million dollars he could, too. And on top of that, I'll throw in a double-sized Cherry Fizz.

Just then I got up—we were both on our knees reexamining the footprints.

"Hey! Brains! Look!"

I pointed down the beach and started running. Brains was kicking up the sand right behind me.

It was the professor. I'd looked up just in time to see him come staggering out of the woods and start running down the beach in our direction.

He was some sight. His clothes were torn, his hair was wild, his glasses, attached to a long black ribbon around his neck were swinging violently from side to side.

"Mine animals! Mine animals! Mine Oscar!" He kept shouting.

He didn't even stop when we reached him. He brushed right between us, running at full speed. He turned off and ran up the path where we had come down from the trailer-zoo.

We were right behind him.

Chapter 4

Night Watchers

The professor kept on running even after he got to the trailer-zoo. His legs kept churning up and down, just like a prize fighter in his corner before the bell rings. He checked the animals on one side of the zoo, counting them, with a "Dot's goot," thrown in every few seconds. Then he scooted around to the other side.

We kept following him, asking questions. But he was much too intent on the safety of his animals to answer us.

Ann had done a good job on calming the animals down. The professor got them all whee-ed up again. Oscar was barking, the crow was cawing and the monkeys were leaping about and chattering.

Then, all of a sudden, the professor chugged off, going back toward the spot where we had found his sandwich paper. He didn't say a word, just chugged off.

Ann, Brains and I chugged right after him. Down the small embankment he went, his hair blowing wildly in the wind. His stocky body was bent forward. The professor knew where he was going. Which was a lot more than we knew.

At the spot along the beach where we had noticed the sand all stirred up by a struggle, the professor darted into the low underbrush back from the beach.

"Ach! Goot! Goot! Goot!" we heard him cry. Then out he came, carrying the wicker creel.

"They didn't got it! They didn't got it!" he said triumphantly.

He sat down suddenly, pulled out a huge red handkerchief and wiped his face and head.

We waited until he got his breath.

"Professor, what happened to you?" Ann asked anxiously.

"We would all appreciate it if you would elucidate," Brains stated.

"Yes, what gives?" I tossed in.

After a few moments, the professor sighed, and said, "Dot Blackie. Dot no good Blackie."

"You refer to the man who was formerly in your employ?" Brains asked. "The young man you had to

discharge a few days ago because he was cruel to your animals?"

"Dot's right. It was Blackie. And another no-gooder with him. Two of them. They attack *me*, the Professor. Never has anything like this happened to me before."

"Start at the beginning, Professor," Brains said. "Tell us all about it. Perhaps we can be of service to you."

I knew it. I knew right then that my vacation was headed for an upset. After all the plans I'd made. I'd saved up plenty of spending money. I'd arranged for Stinky Green to take my paper route for two weeks. And now, here was Brains trying to cut himself in on a mystery.

"We thought you were going to Middlebury, Professor," Ann said. "How did you happen to turn off here?"

"Vell, young lady, like this it is. Mine engagement in Mittleberg, it doesn't start until next Thursday. So, I say to myself, vy don't a nice short vacation I take? On this so beautiful lake? I know about the lake from passing it by once before. Also, on this lake is someone I vant to see. And I am thinking, too, of Oscar. Ach, the vacation will be so vonderful for Oscar. Such goot times he will have swimming. Oscar he loves to swim. And all the time he has only his little tank. But here, a whole big lake he has for the swimming."

"Gee, Professor. That's great," I said. "You sure are nice to your animals."

"Danke schoen," the professor replied.

"That means 'thank you,'" Brains said. I shot him a withering glance. Maybe I didn't know exactly what *danke schoen* meant, but I got the idea. It burned me up, Brains always having to show off his knowledge, especially when it made me look dumber than I am.

"Did Blackie know of your plans for a short vacation on the lake?" Brains asked.

"Ja, ja. He knew. He was going to come with me, until he got so mean to my animals and I had to get rid of him."

Brains' brow furrowed in thought. It was pretty clear that Blackie must have lain in wait for the professor. He must have known about the money in the creel, too.

"So, I see this beautiful spot here along the beach, just after I got a little way past the amusement park," the professor continued. "I say to myself, vy don't I stopping here for a little rest while I have my sandwich. This I do."

"And Blackie and his pal slipped up on you while you were eating?" Brains asked.

"Dot is correct. A big fight we have. I am strong man. Strong as Blackie. But not as strong as Blackie and his friend. But is happen a very funny thing. Blackie takes punch at me. I duck. Blackie's punch hits other feller. Other feller fall down. Blackie trip over him. It is then I toss my creel into the bushes."

"That was quick thinking," I said.

"Yes, but how did you get away from them?" Brains asked.

"While we are fighting, another car pulls up. I heard it. Then down to the beach comes a man, his vife and his two kinder. Blackie sees them. He gets frightened. He runs away. I run away, too. I am mixed up. I run the wrong way, and get lost for a little while in the woods."

"I wonder what happened to the picnickers?" Ann asked.

"Obviously, they were frightened by what they came upon," Brains said, "and quickly decided this was no place for a picnic."

"Well," I said, "All's well that ends well."

"If it has ended," Brains said significantly.

He was still on his detecting kick, I thought to myself.

"One thing more I should like to ask, Professor. When you checked up on the safety of your animals, you seem to have forgotten your mouse, Xenophon."

"Me, forget mine little friend Xenophon! Never!" The professor was indignant. "Here he is. Never do I go anywhere without mine Xenophon." The professor reached into an oversized pocket of his jacket and brought out the waltzing mouse. "You see? Where I go, Xenophon goes."

I happened to look at Ann just about then. She had

taken a step back when Xenophon made his appearance. Then she looked at her watch.

"Oh my! It's getting late. I must get back to camp."

"We can't leave the professor here alone," I said. "Blackie might try another attack."

"I seriously doubt that," Brains said. "I imagine that he will want to formulate other plans."

"Well, whatever, I simply must be going," Ann said. "I'll take you boys to the cottage, then I'll have to hurry along."

"Before you are going, you could maybe tell me where is a cottage called 'By Itself'? Such a funny name," the professor asked.

It was a funny name. But people are always giving their summer cottages crazy names, like "U-N-ME," "We Li-Kit," or "Kum-On-Inn."

But the cottage "By Itself" was well-named all right. I knew where it was, about eight or nine miles east of where we were, just beyond Knob Point. There wasn't another cottage within a mile or more on either side of it.

Brains nodded his head to me, meaning he wanted a whispered conference. I walked over to him.

"I still fear for the professor's safety, Operative Three," he said. "I have a plan. I shall ride with Ann. You ride with the professor. Then, once he is safely in his cottage, and we have settled in ours, we shall come back and carefully inspect the situation."

"But I wanted to go swimming as soon as we got settled," I argued.

"There will be plenty of time for such frivolities, Operative Three. There are more important things at stake just now."

What could I do? I shrugged my shoulders and whispered back, "Okay, Operative X."

We jounced along Lake Shore Road North until we rounded Knob Point and had gone about a mile beyond. It was a good thing I was riding with the professor. He would never have spotted the road leading to his cottage. From the way it looked it hadn't been used all that summer. Grass and weeds had grown over the one-lane road, and it took a sharp eye, a trained investigator's eye, to spot it.

We got the professor settled. It didn't take long. It couldn't, what with Ann dancing around all impatient and bossing everybody. It was getting late, so I couldn't really blame her too much.

Then we went on to the cottage we had rented. It was two miles farther on down the lake. We just dumped all the gear we had brought on the porch, and Ann took off. By the time we had stowed the gear, opened windows, made our beds, turned on the gas, water and electricity, I knew it was getting along toward supper time. My stomach told me so. Brains was all for getting right back to the professor's cottage.

"But Brains. We can't do that. You know what my mother and father would think if we weren't here when they got here."

He did, too. My father likes his meals right on the dot. And if I'm late, as I am much too often, he gets sort of nerved up. I don't mean he gets really riled, but he's quite likely to take a privilege away from me if I'm not on time. A vacation without special privileges is like a sandwich without meat. *Vacation,* I thought, *huh!* My vacation plans were going to split open wider than an atom. I'd known Brains too long.

While we were waiting for my parents, we wandered down to the water.

"Hey, look at that! All painted and ready to go."

I was looking at the 12-foot skiff tied up at the end of the dock. My father had told me that a boat went with the cottage, but this was more than I had expected or hoped for.

We got in the boat and inspected the outboard motor attached to the stern.

"Jeepers. How about that," I said. "A ten-horsepower kicker. I bet it'll push this boat along like a breeze."

"Why don't we try it?" Brains suggested.

That suited me fine. We checked the motor out. The gas tank was full.

We cast off. I took an oar and poled us a few feet away from the dock.

"Okay, Brains, give her a whirl."

Brains took the starter rope, gave one yank, and the motor purred into action on the first pull. Boy, this was going to be great! After a few minutes, I took over. I headed the boat out toward the center of the lake and gave her full throttle. She responded beautifully. I bet we hit fifteen miles an hour.

"This sure beats rowing," I shouted to Brains. He nodded his head and pointed back toward the dock. There was my father waving us in.

Creeps, I couldn't tell from the middle of the lake whether his wave was "friend" or "foe." But he was in a good mood and was all smiles when we pulled alongside.

"How does she work, Jimmy?" he asked.

"Just fine, Dad! Really swell. She's a real tasty boat!"

"Good. Better come along now, your mother has supper about ready. Maybe we can take a spin later."

Brains shot me a glance and shook his head. I knew what he had in mind. He wanted to get back to the professor's as soon as we could after supper.

Well, it was still daylight when we finished eating. Brains and I helped my mother with the dishes. Dad had gone on down to the dock. I heard him call us.

Down to the dock we went. Brains was as fidgety as I am in a dentist's office. He didn't want to go boating. He wanted to go sleuthing.

We went boating. Not for long, though. It was beginning to get dark and my dad's a careful man. We came back into the dock.

"Brains and I want to sort of take a look around, Dad," I said. "We won't be long."

"See that you aren't, Jimmy," he replied, going up the cottage steps. "It's been a long day, and you boys must be tired." He stopped on the top step. "By the way, I ran into your policeman friend, McKeon, this afternoon. He said to tell you he's coming up to the lake with his skin diving gear tomorrow, and if you want to try it out, to meet him about two o'clock at the little private beach just west of here."

"Thanks Dad," I said. He went on inside.

Boy! Skin diving! I was starting to imagine the fun we could have with Officer McKeon's gear, when Brains brought me back with a thump.

"Let's be on our way, Operative Three," he said, heading for the woods. I sighed and followed.

We set off for the professor's cottage on the double. Brains took the lead. He either had cat's eyes, or those glasses he wore were made for night vision. He didn't trip or stumble. He didn't slow up, either.

After the first mile, I called for a halt.

"Creeps, Brains, what are you trying to do—set an Olympic record?" I was panting. "We may need all our strength when we get there, so let's take a breather."

Brains' idea of a breather wouldn't give anyone enough breath to blow out a candle. It seemed to me we had only just stopped when Brains started off again. What could I do? Where Brains Benton leads, Jimmy Carson follows.

We covered the second mile between our cottage and the professor's as fast as we'd covered the first mile. Just before we got to "By Itself," Brains cut off the road and headed for the lake.

"Let's make our approach from the lake side," he whispered. "Someone else might be approaching from the road."

Slipping through those woods at night was a scary business. I bumped into a couple of trees and skinned my knees when I tripped once. Invisible hands seemed to reach out and grab me. Those "hands" were blackberry bushes. They had thorns like needles.

Just as we got to the lakefront, the moon started poking its round, fat face up over the eastern end of the lake. It was a great big orange-colored ball at first. But as we waited, it became smaller and brighter. The tall pine trees cast long shadows. The shadows seemed to dance like witches. "Halloween in July," I muttered to Brains cheerfully.

"Come on, Operative Three," Brains whispered.

He ducked down low and moved slowly toward the professor's cottage.

I was maybe six feet behind him and a little to his right. It looked to me in the moonlight as if the going would be easier on the path I chose. Suddenly, I felt something touch and wrap around my face. I panicked.

"Help! Brains!" I yelled.

Brains turned and leaped back to my side.

"Quiet, Operative Three! Do you want to reveal our position!"

"Someone's trying to smother me," I gasped.

I was pawing at my face frantically. What I found on it made me shiver even more. I had walked right into a great big spider web. Now all I had to do was find the spider. I raked my hands through my hair. I dry-washed my face. I brushed my clothes. No spider. I was sure I could feel it crawling down my back. I whipped off my sweater and T-shirt as if they were on fire.

"Brains, Brains," I said, trying to keep my voice low. "Look at my back. See any spider there?"

I bent over. Brains inspected my back in a ray of moonlight. "It would be impossible to see a spider in this light."

"Where's your flashlight?" I squeaked at him.

"I dropped it this afternoon while I was unpacking. The bulb was broken," he muttered.

"So, I've got illumination." I'd remembered the book of paper matches my mother had given me to light the pilot light of the gas stove back in the cottage. "Here," I said, frantically handing the matchbook to him. "Light one and take a look."

I bent over. Brains struck a match and inspected my back.

"There is nothing there, Operative Three. You are allowing your imagination too full a play." He handed me back the matches and I shoved them into my pocket.

From the tone of his voice, I knew he was pretty upset by my actions. I knew I could have given our position away. But I'm a town boy. Those woods and spiders and all sorts of strange things—ugh—I was all for getting out of there. I said so, too. But not Brains.

"We are on a mission of mercy, Operative Three," he said. "We must make certain the professor is safe. Come."

Well, I followed him, still wondering where that spider had gone. Where there's a spider web, there's got to be a spider, I insisted. I had the spider web; parts of it were still clinging to my hair. I just hoped the spider had vamoosed.

We crept through the woods toward the professor's house. When we came to the edge of the clearing surrounding the cottage, Brains dropped down on his hands and knees. I did the same.

The cottage was all lighted up. We could hear the professor singing away at the top of his voice. Now and then the song was punctuated by a bark from Oscar.

"He's okay," I whispered, "Let's get out of here."

"Not yet. We'll wait a while."

I could hear my heart pounding. I could hear weird noises coming from every side. That woods was full of noises. Not loud ones, but muffled, strange, scary ones.

How long we stayed there, I don't want to think about. Seemed like hours to me. I was tingling and itching all over. I felt there must be a million crawling things that had decided my body was a summer camp. I decided that Brains or no Brains, I was getting out of there. I reached out my hand to touch his shoulder.

"Shsssh," he hissed at me.

Then I heard it, too. Somewhere behind us, I heard a twig snap, then another. We were just off the path that led down to the professor's dock. We were well concealed.

More twigs snapped. Someone—or something—was coming up that path. If it was an animal, it was a big one. Lake Carmine wild life, I knew, was generally medium-to small-sized.

One of my hands grasped Brains' shoulder. We huddled together. I could hear his breath coming in short, excited gasps. He wasn't any calmer than I was. Just as scared, too, I bet.

I could hear frogs croaking. There were peeps and beeps from other nocturnal wild life. From off down the lake came the eerie screech of an owl. A mosquito whined in my ear.

Brains pulled me closer to him. I saw him staring toward the path. I looked, too.

A man stood at the edge of the clearing. His body was outlined in the moonlight, his face was in a shadow. He just stood there, motionless.

Chapter 5

To the Rescue!

Was I ever wrong about Brains being scared!

We were still huddled together, the two of us, our two pairs of wide eyes never wavering a second from that figure in the shadows. He stood there like an Indian, absolutely quiet, absolutely motionless, spying on the cottage.

After several minutes—after several *hours*, it seemed— he turned his head in our direction. Honest, I thought I could feel his eyes burning into mine. I was sure he had spotted us.

He hadn't. His head pivoted back. The night watcher resumed his spying on the professor's cottage.

Would he ever leave? More important, would *we* ever leave? We certainly couldn't as long as he stood there. I didn't have any hankering to tangle with a grown man in a dark woods.

Not Brains, though. Even as I huddled there quivering like jelly, that ever-active mind of Brains' was spinning out a plan. And what a plan! When I heard the plan, I thought the president of the Benton and Carson International Detective Agency had not only flipped his lid, he'd tossed it into the deepest hole in Lake Carmine. I heard that plan almost right away—just as soon as the silent watcher moved. He moved along the edge of the clearing, still keeping in the shadows, but we could still see him silhouetted against patches of moonlight that filtered through the trees.

I felt Brains tug at my arm and he moved his head close to mine.

"Now's our chance, Operative Three," he whispered.

"Great. Let's get out of here," I whispered in reply and started to crawl backward. Brains tightened his hold on my arm.

"No. We can't leave now. We've got to make certain who that watcher is."

"It's got to be Blackie, hasn't it?" I asked.

"Perhaps. Perhaps not. But at any rate, we must seize this opportunity to get a closer look at the man. We must know what he looks like."

Some opportunity, I thought. A great opportunity to get knocked on the noggin. I could think of lots of other things I'd prefer doing with that opportunity. If opportunity was going to knock, I didn't want it knocking on me.

"Here's my plan," Brains continued. "I've got a rock here. I'm going to toss it back down the path—over that way." He pointed to a spot behind us where the path led to the lake.

"When that man comes charging down the path to investigate, you are to catch him in the spotlight."

"Spotlight!" I nearly howled. "We haven't even got a flashlight, not even a ma . . ." My voice petered out like a tired siren.

"Precisely. You have a packet of matches and we shall use them like a torch."

"This little old bunch of paper nothing is going to be a *torch*?" I asked. "You're kidding."

"Think," Brains snapped. "When book matches are alight at the same time, they flare—briefly but brilliantly. You are to toss the lighted packet toward him. Be careful."

"Great," I muttered and tried to do it sarcastically. "When my father accidentally ignited a whole book of matches once, he yowled like a burnt cat."

Maybe I wasn't whispering loud enough. Anyway, Brains didn't pay any attention to me. He raised up and heaved that rock. It landed just where he wanted it to. I told you he was a fine baseball pitcher.

That rock landed with a large thump, and at the same time a large lump landed in my throat. I looked up. Sure enough, our silent watcher was making fast tracks in our direction.

Well, here goes James MacDonald Carson, I said to myself. Mine not to reason why, mine but to spotlight a spy and not burn myself in the try.

The night watcher sped toward us. He rounded the corner onto the path without slackening his pace. I was on the ready, one match loose and set to strike on the rough surface. My fingers were shaking and for one wild minute I thought I'd miss the striking surface by a mile. But I scratched, held the packet by the outer corner, set fire to the whole book and—pitched it.

The torch streaked through the night gloom toward the man. Startled, he stopped dead in his tracks for just the merest breath of a second, but long enough for me to see him. Then he raced down the path.

"I saw his face!" Brains shouted. "After him!"

I just groaned. I'd had enough. But Brains started loping down the path, and I felt I just had to go along.

The prowler led us a merry chase. We would gain on him for a little while, then lose him. Brains fell once, tripping over a fallen tree trunk. What Brains could do, I could do. Only when I tripped, it was my luck to land smack in a briar-filled thicket. I let out a howl that must have made the night animals feel they'd been invaded by Martians.

When I stopped howling and scrambled out of the briars, the prowler was too far away for us to continue our pursuit. We could still hear him thrashing through the underbrush, but the sounds grew fainter and fainter. After a few more minutes, we heard the sound of a car being started some distance away. Our night watcher had fled.

"Are you all right, Operative Three?" Brains asked.

"Oh, sure. I'm just full of bruises and scratches and torn clothing. Think nothing of it."

Brains ignored my sarcasm. "We can congratulate ourselves on a good night's work," he said.

"I don't see that we did anything so great."

"We frightened off a would-be attacker, did we not? We prevented a possible attack on the professor. I consider that a very definite accomplishment."

I wasn't in any mood or condition to argue. I just wanted to get out of that woods, home and into my bed. Brains had one more idea, though. He wanted to make a final check on the professor's cottage. I followed him back up the path. When we got to the clearing, we saw just the outline of the cottage. The lights had been turned out. Either the professor had been frightened by our racket out in the woods, or he had gone to bed.

Tired, with my body aching as if I'd been scrimmaging against the Chicago Bears, I took the lead in heading for home.

It was nearly ten o'clock when we got there. My father had gone to bed. But Mom was still up, reading, and waiting for us. We came in the back door and went right to our room.

"Is that you, Jimmy?" Mother called out. "You're late. Are you and Barclay all right?"

"Yes, Mom," I sang out. "Just tired. We're going right to bed."

"Sweet dreams," she sang back.

After the nightmare we'd just gone through, any dream would have seemed sugar-coated.

At breakfast the next morning, my father announced he was going to call on a friend, Dick Hubbell who lived about half a mile away on Trysting Path.

"Will it be all right if Brains and I go out in the boat?" I asked.

"If your mother hasn't anything for you to do."

I looked at Mom hopefully.

"I don't know of anything," she said, and I let out a soft sigh of thanks. You see, the first thing Brains had said to me when we woke up, even before we were out of bed, was that we'd have to get right back over to the professor's. He wanted to make sure that night prowler hadn't come back.

I wanted to take the boat out. It would be a lot easier to get to the professor's by water than through that briar-infested woods.

So, right after we'd helped Mom do the breakfast dishes, Brains and I set out in the skiff to visit Professor Gus.

The trip on the lake by boat was about a mile and a half. The cottage "By Itself" is just east of Knob Point, in a kind of bay. From our cottage we could skim across the bay formed by the point. It was much longer on foot.

The outboard was purring along smoothly. We made the trip in about ten minutes.

As I slowed down to make a landing at the rickety dock that jutted out from the beach in front of Professor Gus' cottage, I asked Brains what plans he had made for this visit.

"Primarily to ascertain the professor's safety," he replied in a solemn voice.

"I just hope, then, that you don't expect us to spend every day body-guarding the professor."

"We will give him all the protection he needs. Remember, he is only staying until next Wednesday."

I had forgotten that. It made me feel better. I knew that as long as the professor was on the lake, Brains wouldn't rest until he got himself neck deep in the prof's affairs.

We tied up to the dock and took the path up to the cottage. I shuddered as we passed the spot where we'd lain in hiding the night before and where I had been the boy flame-thrower.

The trailer-zoo was parked by the side of the cottage. We could hear the animals, all except Oscar the seal. I figured he must be taking an early morning nap in his nice cool tank. That made me think of swimming. It was getting hot already.

We hopped up the three steps leading to the porch and knocked on the screen door. No answer. We could see inside, but there was no sign of life. We knocked again, louder. Still no answer. We walked around the house to the back door, the one nearest the road. We didn't get any answer there, either.

"Let's take a closer look at the trailer," I said. "Maybe the professor's in there, looking after his animals."

"A very good suggestion, Operative Three."

Brains was still calling me by my code name which told me he considered himself on a case—as if I hadn't known it all along. I just didn't want to admit it completely. This was supposed to be a vacation.

I was looking in through the window at the front end of the trailer. Brains had gone around to the rear. I didn't see the professor but I also didn't notice anything else unusual. Brains did though. He called me and I hurried around to the rear to join him.

"Oscar is gone," he said.

My excitement rose like a kite in a strong March wind.

"The professor gone! Oscar gone! Blackie's been here!"

Brains frowned. "I think not," he said, not a bit excited. "You will recall, Operative Three, that one reason the professor wanted to stay a few days at the lake was so that Oscar could go swimming."

"Oh, yes," I said sheepishly, remembering.

"And when we tied up at the dock—did you notice anything missing?"

I thought hard. It didn't get me anywhere though.

"You should have," Brains said. "You know that some kind of a boat goes along with the rental of all summer cottages. There was no boat at the dock when we landed, was there?"

Now I remembered. How could I miss anything as big as a boat. I guess this was going to be another one of my bad mornings.

"From the absence of the professor, Oscar, and the boat, I'd say the professor has taken Oscar swimming."

I could have figured the same thing out just as easily. Only Brains is thinking all the time about detecting. I am, too, most of the time, but I just couldn't get myself down to business. I was going to soon, though.

"So, let's go out on the lake and locate the professor. I should think it would be most entertaining to watch a seal cavorting in Lake Carmine."

We went back to the boat and headed out. We scanned the lake carefully, but couldn't spot any rowboat with a wild-haired professor and a swimming seal.

Then, as we rounded Knob Point, we got action. Plenty of it. About a quarter of a mile away, we saw two boats. One was a small rowboat. The other was a speedboat with two men in it. The speedboat was circling the rowboat. Twice we saw it dart in, striking at the smaller boat like a dog attacking a small animal.

"Full speed ahead, Operative Three!" Brains shouted. "It must be the professor!"

Chapter 6

A Drowned Fortune

I gave the motor full throttle. We shot ahead. Our bow cut a deep wake. The water rushed by. Brains was leaning forward in the bow of the boat, his neck stretched out like a stork in flight.

It was the professor all right. We could see that clearly enough as we sped nearer. And there was no doubt that he was under attack. That speedboat made two more passes at the professor's boat as we narrowed the distance between us and danger.

When we were still about one hundred yards away, the attackers in the speedboat spotted us. We must have scared them. They swung away from the rowboat and sped toward the western end of the lake with their motor roaring.

I throttled down the motor and we pulled up alongside Professor Gus' rowboat.

"I am safed!" he cried out and sank down on the stern seat. He had lost both oars and was drifting helplessly. All of a sudden I jumped a foot and almost went overboard. Two loud barks did it to me. All I could think of was, what was a dog doing that far out in the lake? Then I spotted Oscar the seal, swishing about in the water, leaping and diving, but not in play. If a seal can have an angry expression on its whiskered face, Oscar had one. He looked stern and indignant.

Brains scrambled out of our boat into the professor's. He placed a hand on the old gentleman's shoulder to comfort him.

"Neffer, neffer, neffer," moaned the professor, "have such bad things happened to me."

"They've gone now, Professor Gus. We're here to protect you. You can also count on our professional services," Brains continued, "We'll protect you from Blackie. It was Blackie, I assume, who engineered the attack?"

"Ya. It was Blackie all right. To think that once I took him in. I fed him and bought him his clothes. I gave him a bed. And now, it is my hand that fed him he bites."

Professor Gus' chin was on his chest, his long white hair falling over his face.

"What do we do now?" I called to Brains.

"There aren't any oars in this boat. See if you can find them."

"What happened to them, Professor?" I called out.

"I use them to fight off dot Blackie. First I drop one, then I lose the other one."

I put my boat in low speed and started circling the professor's rowboat. I kept widening my circles, and on the third time around, I found one oar. I found the other one on my fourth circuit.

When I got back to Professor Gus' boat, Brains had the situation well in hand.

"The professor is much too tired and distraught to row. We'll tow him home. Catch this rope." Brains tossed the painter to me and I looped it through a large eye-screw in the stern of our boat.

Just as we were about to get under way, Oscar the seal, who had been splashing all around us, suddenly leaped out of the water and into the boat with Brains and the professor. Oscar was sore. He set up a terrific yapping.

"What's the matter with that seal?" I called back.

"He is hungry," the professor answered. "So hungry from all the swimming yet. And I have nothing to give him. Poor Oscar. Mine poor seal."

"Where's the creel?" Brains asked. "I thought you always carried it with you."

"I did. I did. But now, dot creel is gone. It is on bottom of the lake."

"On the bottom!" Brains and I shouted together.

"Ya. On the bottom. Oscar's food is gone."

"And all that money is gone, too," I said.

"Was the money still in the creel?" Brains asked.

"Ya, the money and Oscar's food."

Creeps, the professor seemed to be more worried about Oscar's herring than he was about all that money.

"But what happened to the creel, Professor? How did it get lost overboard?"

"I did it. I lost it. I know when I see Blackie coming that it is mine money he wants, mine creel. So, I loop strap around place where I grip oar, hidden under mine hand so he cannot see it. I put creel over side of boat hanging in the water. I hold tight to the oar and the strap—so." The professor took the oar and demonstrated. Sure enough, he could have concealed the strap from Blackie on that side of the boat.

"What happened then?" Brains and I said almost at the same time.

"Blackie, he get very angry when I say I have hidden the creel far, far away. He tries to come into my boat. I grab one oar and—thwack—I hit him a good one with it. But the other oar—ach, I forget. It is the oar with the creel on it. I let it go, so mad I was. The creel is heavy. It pulls out the oar from the rowing place. Down it sinks."

"Did Blackie see it go?" Brains asked.

"Nein. He is still so mad from the wallop I give him, he gets back into his boat and—zoom—he tries to break me into little pieces with it." The professor's voice had become very excited as he acted out the battle. Now it changed and became sad again. "But the creel is gone now," he added, "is gone forever."

Jeepers, all that money at the bottom of Lake Carmine!

"Ve home go now, please," the professor said. "So sad I feel. Dot money—gone, and not even mine was it."

"What do you mean, Professor?" Brains asked, suspiciously. "Back in Crestwood, you told us it *was* your money."

"Nein. No, dot money was for somebody else. Please no more do ve talk about it. Only to mine cottage I want to go now. Mine animals, they miss me."

The professor was a funny duck. Here he had just lost several thousand dollars—money that didn't belong to him—but his animals came first. Well, I figured, maybe he had more where that came from.

"Okay, Jimmy," Brains called out, "Let's go." Brains must have decided Professor Gus was too upset to question him further. I put the motor in gear and the line between the two boats tightened. Brains got in the stern of the professor's boat and used one oar as a rudder to keep the following boat from veering.

We must have made quite a picture as we chugged

back toward shore. There I was, towing a boat carrying a sad, white-haired professor, a thoughtful, skinny red-head and a yapping seal.

When we got back to "By Itself," the first thing the professor did was get Oscar some dried fish. Then he fed the rest of his zoo. He went about these chores in silence. Not once did he speak to Brains or me. He didn't even have his usual cheery words for his animals. Old Gustave was feeling low. Who could blame him?

We watched quietly. We weren't very happy either. I noticed Brains was tugging away at that left ear lobe of his, pinching it between his thumb and forefinger. I knew what that meant. Brains was thinking. Brains was laying plans.

I nudged Brains. "We'd better go. Dad will be home by now. He may want to use the boat."

Brains nodded his head.

"We must be going, Professor," Brains said. "But we'll be near at hand if you need us."

"Ach! Danke schoen . . . thank you, mine boys. You have saved me from dot Blackie. Neffer can I repay you."

"Oh, that's all right, Professor," I said. "Don't you even think about that. We don't want any pay—we just don't want Blackie to rob you."

"Vell, he can't rob me now. There is no more the money to be taken."

"About that money, Professor," Brains said. "I think we can get it back."

"Get it back? Mine money!" The professor was astounded. "Dot money is on bottom of lake. Deep water. You can't get it back."

"Don't be too sure of that, Professor," Brains replied. "The firm of Benton and Carson specialize in recovering lost objects."

In twenty-five feet of water, I thought. Some of that water must have soaked into my partner's head.

"Vell, if you can get back the money yet, it vould be wunderbar, but . . ." The professor was skeptical.

We said good-by and headed for the dock.

"What's all this noise about getting the professor's money back," I asked as we got into our boat.

"Oh, that?" Brains answered vaguely. "That's not what's bothering me."

"Not bothering you! What are you talking about!" I was indignant. That money was in a good twenty-five or thirty feet of water. And here Brains is saying in his offhand manner that he wasn't bothered about how to get it back.

"No, recovering the money isn't what's worrying me."

"Well then, just what is?" I demanded.

"I am mystified by another remark the professor made. You will recall, Operative Three, that the professor said the money wasn't his?"

I remembered all right.

"If the money belonged to someone else, then the professor could be in really serious trouble. Whoever that money belongs to is going to want it. He could make lots of trouble for the professor."

"You don't think the professor stole . . . I mean . . ." Creeps, I couldn't believe the professor had come by that money illegally. "I can't imagine that nice old man doing anything dishonest."

"Nor can I," Brains said. "But it is a real puzzler. And the only way to solve the puzzle is to get that money back."

"Oh, sure," I said sarcastically. "We'll just go back there and I'll dive down and get it, since I used to be a pearl diver in Samoa."

"Operative Three, that is exactly what you are going to do," Brains replied, calm as a fat cat sleeping in the sun.

"What!" I yowled. "I'm going to dive down and get that money!"

"Precisely. And now, as you suggested, I think we had better be getting back. You said your father may be waiting."

Chapter 7

SCUBA

Dad was on the dock, waiting impatiently for us to return. I was just as impatient for an explanation from Brains about my diving down for the professor's money. He wouldn't say a word about it on our way back.

"About time you boys got back," Dad humphed. "You can't monopolize this boat."

"I'm sorry, Dad. We didn't mean to be gone so long." Dad wasn't really sore. He just wanted the boat.

"Dick Hubbell and I want to go out and do a little fishing. I told him I'd pick him up about noon. It's after twelve now. You lads beat it up to the house. Your mother has your lunch ready."

Dad stowed his gear in the boat and I pushed it off for him. Brains and I went into the house.

Mom had roast beef sandwiches for us, left over from last night's roast. My favorite. Mom was eating a dish of Jello and a glass of milk called "Slenderette." It was milk with all the cream taken out of it. I'd tasted it once. Might as well drink a glass of water with chalk coloring. My mother, you may gather, is a diet bug. She's always trying something new she reads in those women's magazines, or something someone had told her about at one of her club meetings.

Right after our lunch, I nailed Brains. I pinned him down. I grilled him.

"Now, Operative X," I said, fixing him with my sternest expression. "Just what is this Operative-Three-diving-for-money-business?"

"Officer McKeon should be at the lake by now," was his reply.

"So?"

"We are to meet him at two o'clock, you will recall."

"I recall."

"And you will also recall that he was going to demonstrate the art of skin diving for us . . ."

A light flickered in my dark little mind.

"Now hold it, Operative X . . . If you think I'm going to learn how to skin dive . . ." I spluttered.

"Why, Operative Three! I'm surprised at you. I

thought surely, anyone who loves water and swimming as much as you do ... why I was positive you'd beg our friend McKeon to teach you how."

Well, how about that? I thought to myself. I was all ready to argue with Brains, no matter what he said. And here I was, talking myself out of a good thing. Of course I wanted to learn how to skin dive. "What's the matter with you, Carson?" I asked myself.

Out loud I said: "That's a great idea, Operative X. Gosh, I don't know what I must have been thinking about."

"Of course, while I don't have the same love of water that surges through your veins, I have no deep aversion to it. So, I suppose I might as well acquire the art of skin diving at the same time."

Just like that! Brains is going to pick up skin diving while designing a build-it-yourself atom smasher at the same time. And, you know, I believe he could do just that. What Brains wants to learn, he learns; and quickly, too.

"Gee, and another thing," I had a new thought. "Maybe Officer McKeon can help us do something about Blackie."

"I doubt that, Operative Three. Here on Lake Carmine, Officer McKeon is beyond his jurisdictional authority. An act more overt than those perpetrated thus far would have to take place."

"Overt?"

"I mean an act more open to view. An act of violence, an act against society—a clear-cut breaking of the criminal code."

"Gosh, aren't Blackie's two attacks on the professor overt enough?"

"No, I don't believe they are—not thus far. You must remember, Operative Three, that we have only the professor's word for the first attack . . ."

"That's good enough for me," I cut in.

"For you, yes, and also for me. But, I doubt if the attack could be proven in a court of law. As for the second attack, the one we came upon down the lake, was any harm done?"

"Any harm done! Creeps, what about the money?"

"And just who was it who dropped the money?"

Brains had me again. The professor had lost the money. Oh, sure, Blackie had attacked him by boat, and the professor had been forced by the attack to drop the money, but, as Brains said, could any crime be proven against Blackie? It would be Professor Gus' word against his—and that of his companion in the boat.

We knew, of course, that Blackie was at the bottom of all the trouble. But I knew we'd have a tough time trying to convince the authorities of Blackie's guilt. There just wasn't anything overt enough to prove—not yet.

"It is my considered opinion, Operative Three, that

until we can assemble more concrete evidence against Blackie, that the wisest course for us to pursue is to remain silent about the matter for the present. However, we shall continue to press forward—we will eventually bring Blackie to justice."

I sure hoped so, but right then, I didn't know how.

We left our cottage and walked along the lake shore toward a private beach, about half a mile away, where Dad had said we were to meet Officer McKeon. He was a nut on this skin diving business. On every day off he had, he came out to Lake Carmine and spent most of the day under water.

He was good, too. We'd seen him work before. On the "Stolen Dummy" case, he had plunged into Boiling Pond and worked around a submerged automobile.

Officer McKeon was waiting for us at the beach.

He greeted us with a big grin and a bigger wise-crack. "How are Sherlock Holmes and Doctor Watson this fine day? I bet the *Ledger* will soon be carrying another headline about you two. Know how it will read? Like this:

KIDS KAPTURE KRIMINAL ON KARMINE

"All words beginning with the letter 'K.' Get it?"

"We 'get it,'" Brains replied. I could see he didn't take very much to Officer McKeon's kidding. But

McKeon is a good policeman. Oh, sure, he kids us a lot, but he also has plenty of respect for our sleuthing abilities. We'd worked with him on several cases, and he knew we could deliver.

"Well now," he continued. "How about a dip in the deep? Either of you two want to learn how to skin dive?"

"I do," I said.

"For the moment, I shall observe," Brains said.

"Okay—here's my gear—called SCUBA. . . ."

"Scuba? What's that mean?" I asked.

"Self-Contained Underwater Breathing Apparatus," Brains replied. "The first letter of each word forms. . . ."

"Say, sleuth, how do you happen to know that?" McKeon cut in with a surprised voice.

"Oh, I make it my business to keep abreast of modern trends," Brains answered. "I have a book on skin diving."

"Well knock me down with a feather!" McKeon said. I could tell he was impressed.

McKeon had his skin diving equipment carefully laid out on a blanket.

"Now, here's the equipment we use. It's all been tested. That's important. Equipment should first be tested in a swimming pool. And it must be thoroughly checked out every time it's used and before it's used, of course. Skin diving is fun—when you are careful."

"Here are three important rules: 1. Never dive without a companion along. 2. Be sure you know how to clear your mask. 3. Be absolutely positive you have the type weight belt that you can jettison at once. That's in case you get into trouble under water and have to surface. And if that ever does happen, don't panic and surface too rapidly—don't come up any faster than the ascent rate of the escaping air bubbles."

I was really interested in all this. I could tell that Officer McKeon was a good and careful instructor. Brains was interested, too, but he had read all about the things McKeon was explaining.

"Now, here's the face mask." He picked it up and put it on. "If water gets on the inside, you won't be able to see. Here's how you clear it." McKeon lay down on his back. "In the water, you'd roll over on your back. Then blow air out through your nose. The air pressure will force the water out around the edges of the mask."

McKeon got up. "Understand that, Jimmy? And you, Brains?"

We both nodded our heads.

"Now see this belt? It has weights on it. Lead weights. You have to take weights off and put them on until they just balance your own natural buoyancy. This belt is just right for me. The most important thing about any weight belt is how it buckles on. Always be sure it has a safety release buckle. I'll show you what I mean."

Officer McKeon strapped on the weight belt.

"Now you see how I put the strap through the

buckle? One fast flip of my hand, and the belt is released. I don't have to fool around and waste time trying to undo a buckle. But, if you hooked the strap through a buckle as you do an ordinary belt, you'd have to tug it out to release the belt. You try it, Jimmy."

I did, and it worked fine.

"Now here's the air tank—holds enough compressed air for one hour. Then there's an emergency supply of two minutes. You can hit the emergency supply with a fast slap at this lever. But you'll probably never need it. Handy to have, though, if you stay down too long."

Officer McKeon strapped the tank on his back, put on his flippers and mask and waded out waist-deep. We followed him in. He stuck the mouthpiece of the air hose into his mouth and went down. He did this several times, staying down from two to five minutes.

"Want to try it now, Jimmy?"

"I sure do."

He juggled the weights on the belt and I climbed into the gear. Well, believe me, talk about fun! This skin diving is really something. Specially if you have a good instructor like Officer McKeon.

I used the equipment for about half an hour, then Brains had himself checked out in it.

"Good pupils, both of you," McKeon said, and I could tell he really meant it.

"Tell you what," he said, "let's go out in the rowboat

and make a few dives in deeper water."

We did. We spent about three hours with McKeon supervising us. I stayed down one time for ten full minutes. Brains' longest dive was five. McKeon had us try out everything—release the weight belt, hit the emergency air supply valve—the works. He didn't miss a single trick in training us. And he made sure we did everything with great care.

"That's all for today, boys. Lesson's over. I've got to get back to Crestwood."

"When will you be out again?" I asked.

"Let's see—I'm working a mixed-up schedule this month. Everybody seems to want to take his vacation in July. So I'm working what we call the swing shift. I swing around from one day to another—substituting for the other officers who are away. For the next two weeks, my two days off are Saturday—today—and Thursday. So, I'll be back out here Thursday."

Brains was thinking.

"What's puzzling you, Brains?" McKeon asked.

"I was wondering—wouldn't it be easier for you if you left your skin diving equipment at our cottage? Then you wouldn't have to lug it back and forth."

Officer McKeon grinned. "You mean you'd like to have the use of it when I'm not here at the lake?"

Brains nodded his head, and I chimed in with an eager: "We sure would! Is it all right with you?"

"I guess so. But remember—always be careful. And never dive unless you're together—one of you in the boat at all times."

We promised. It was an easy promise to make. I liked diving all right. It was fun to inspect the lake bottom and see fish swimming past you. You feel like a king-size fish yourself. But I know that when I was down in the deep, I wanted someone upstairs keeping an eye on me.

It was nearly supper time when we got back to our cottage.

"Tomorrow," Brains announced, "we go after the professor's money."

"Yo-ho-ho and a bottle of Cherry Fizz," I sang out. "We dive for sunken treasure."

Brains gave me a beady-eyed look. "Correction," he said. "We dive to see that justice is done."

Chapter 8

Solo Assignment

Next morning, after breakfast, we were all set to practice skin diving. We had to wait an hour, though. Mom saw to that.

"You boys know that it isn't safe to go swimming until an hour after you've eaten," she said.

So, we waited the hour, watching the clock as every minute ticked off. We spent the time checking out the equipment as Officer McKeon had showed us.

We took the skiff and went about a hundred feet off the dock. Both Mom and Dad stood on the dock to watch us. We dropped anchor in eighteen feet of water, and I donned the equipment. Over the side I went, and sank down to the bottom. Everything worked fine. I stayed down about ten minutes. The bottom of the lake at this spot was great for skin diving. It was solid sand, no mud to kick up and cloud the water as I moved along the bottom.

When I surfaced, my father was in the boat. He had put on his swim trunks and swum out.

"Your mother was worried, Jimmy," he said. "You shouldn't have stayed down so long the first time. She's never seen anyone dive before, so naturally she got worried when you didn't come right back up. Matter of fact, I felt a little shaky about you myself."

"Gee, I'm sorry, Dad. But everything was just fine. You ought to try it yourself sometime."

"Maybe I'll just do that," he said, laughing. Then he dove over the side and swam back to the dock.

Brains took a trial dive next. He didn't stay down as long as I did. We clowned around the rest of the morning, swimming, diving, and just scooting around the lake in the boat. After our big mid-day meal, we decided to boat over to the professor's. Dad just grunted when I asked him if he minded if we used the boat that afternoon. He was buried behind the Sunday paper. It would take him all afternoon to read it.

The professor was overjoyed to see us.

"Ach! Mine friends! Mine goot friends. So happy am I to see you."

"We have a plan, Professor," Brains announced. "And we need your help to put it into action."

"Anything I can do for you goot boys, I do with the most pleasure. Vat is it you are vanting?"

"Well," Brains continued, "we thought we would try to locate the money you dropped into the lake."

"And how can you do that?"

"We've got skin diving equipment, Professor," I cut in. "We can go down to the bottom and search for the creel."

"Skin diving equipment? Please, I am not understanding."

Brains and I gave the professor a short lecture on what skin diving was. I don't think he understood too much of it. And what he did understand, I doubt if he believed. But he was only too anxious to go along with us. He wanted that money back.

"So, if you boys say it is all right, then I go with you." He paused, and his eyes brightened up. "Maybe ve could take mine Oscar along?"

"Sure, Professor. We'll be glad to."

Oscar flopped down the trail with us and plunged into the lake. We got into our boat and set out towards Knob Point. Oscar swam along with us. Sometimes he'd leap ahead, dive and come up right alongside the boat. Twice he circled us, diving and barking, and having himself the time of a seal's life.

"Have you any idea, Professor, about where you dropped the creel overboard?" Brains asked.

"Not too goot, I'm afraid," Professor Gus answered. A frown creased his heavy face. He raised his right hand to shade his eyes and searched the shore line.

"I know that I row toward dot point. Oscar is with me. After a while, I put down the oars and just drift along. Is so pleasant. The sun was brightly shining. I am nice and warm. The water is so pretty. Then, all of a sudden, dot Blackie comes at me out of the nowhere."

"Can you remember about where you were when you first sighted Blackie?" I asked.

"Did you happen to look at the shore to establish a landmark?" Brains asked.

"It was somewhere along here. A breeze is blowing, and it is blowing me right past that point over there."

The professor indicated the tip of Knob Point.

"I pick up the oars when I see Blackie. I start rowing very fast. I think if I can get inside that point and near to the shore by, then maybe Blackie can't follow me."

Brains and I knew that the professor had had his water battle with Blackie west of the point. We remembered that when we had set out to find him the day before, we hadn't sighted his boat until we had rounded the point.

I was at the tiller of our boat. I started circling.

"Professor, when you think I'm about at the spot where you dropped the creel overboard, holler out," I said.

"I vill. Dot I vill," he replied.

We cruised around for about ten minutes.

"Stop! Stop the boat," the professor shouted.

I did.

"Here, I think. Somewhere about here," the professor said. "I can not be sure, of course, but not too far away from this spot, is where the money is on the lake bottom."

"Heave the anchor over, Brains," I called out.

The anchor hit the water with a splash, and the rope played out some twenty-five feet. While Brains secured the boat, I put on the skin diving equipment.

"I'll give it a try, Brains," I said. "I want to see what the bottom's like."

"Let's trust it isn't muddy," Brains said.

"Yes. That's what I'm afraid of. If it's muddy, we're in trouble."

I slipped over the side of the boat and went straight down. The bottom was patchy. There were places where it was fine white sand, then spots where the sand greyed off into a thin layer of mud. I roamed around, looking up every now and then to make certain I hadn't wandered too far away from the boat. I could see it silhouetted against the bright sunlight above.

It was really interesting walking around on the bottom of the lake, twenty-five feet below the surface. But I didn't find what I was looking for. I guess I must have stayed down nearly twenty minutes.

When I surfaced, there was an eager, excited and questioning look on the professor's face. I took off my face mask and shook my head.

"Nothing, Jimmy?" Brains asked.

"Not a thing. I covered quite an area, too. The bottom's not too bad. I think if the creel is around there, we'll be able to spot it."

"Too bad. Too bad," the professor said. "But maybe you could again try?" he asked hopefully.

"Not right now, Professor. This air tank only holds an hour's supply. We used it yesterday and this morning. I don't think there's enough air left to make another try today. I know I don't want to try it."

"But don't give up hope, Professor," Brains said. "We can get the tank refilled at Wonder Park. And I still have another idea that should help us locate the creel."

This was news to me. My partner hadn't confided any other idea to me. But that was like Brains. He didn't come up with his ideas until he was ready to put them into effect. I was dying to know what the new idea was.

We cruised down to Wonder Park where they have a high-pressure compressor and refilled the air tank. Then we dropped the professor off, and headed for home. We'd been gone most of the afternoon, and supper time wasn't far off.

"What's this other idea you've got, Operative X?" I asked. "Give out with some information."

Brains was in deep thought. I asked my question again.

"We need an underwater metal detector. We can't continue our unscientific method of searching."

"And just where are you going to dream up an underwater metal detector?" I asked.

"Perhaps I already have, Operative Three. You will recall the device I inspected in the Crime Lab when we stopped for a few minutes on our way out here?"

"You mean that thing that looked like a vacuum cleaner?"

"That's right, Operative Three. I had been working on it for several days. I thought such a mechanism might be fun to use here on the lake, searching the bottom. I had no idea, of course, that it would ever be put to a practical use."

"Gee, that's great! Real great!" Then it struck me. The metal detector was in the Crime Lab in Crestwood. And Crestwood was twenty-five miles away.

"But how are we going to get it, Operative X?"

Brains didn't have any answer for that. My father did, though.

That night, right after supper, Dad came to our rescue. He didn't know it, but for once he was a big help to the firm of Benton and Carson, private eyes, instead of being critical of our operations.

"Clara," he said to my mother, "I've got to go into Crestwood tomorrow."

"Oh, John," that's my father's name, "Must you interrupt your vacation the very first day it starts? Just why in the world do you have to go into town?"

"Well, I left a few matters that I want to get out of the way. Just some odds and ends at the gas company." My father is head accountant at the Crestwood Gas and Appliance Company. "If I don't do them, they'll be in the back of my mind for the rest of our vacation."

"I don't suppose you'll also find time for a round of golf while you're there," Mom put in, and there was no escaping her wry tone.

"Well, Clara, I do have to have lunch with Bert Thomas." Either my father didn't catch that sarcastic note, or if he did, he decided to ignore it. "And since Bert and I usually do play Saturdays . . ."

"And since you didn't get to play yesterday," Mom cut in.

"Why yes, since we missed our usual Saturday round, why I thought if Bert were free, we might get in a fast eighteen holes."

When it comes to putting first things first, my father puts his golf game high on the list. Mom just shrugged.

"All right, dear," she said, "I know the gas company couldn't do without you tomorrow."

"Now, Clara," Dad said.

"Mr. Carson, I wonder if I could go into Crestwood with you?" Brains asked.

"Why certainly, Barclay. But I should think you'd want to spend every minute you could here on the lake."

"Oh, I do, sir. But there's an instrument at my laboratory I want to do some work on. I expect to bring it back here for final testing and use."

My father frowned at this. He knew how Brains was always working on some scientific device or other, and quite often he had said, "That Benton boy is going to blow himself up some day. And our Jimmy will go right along with him." This time, though, he remained silent, except to say it was okay for Brains to go along with him.

They left early the next morning. But not until Brains had taken me aside and given me my orders for the day.

"Operative Three," he said. "You know why I have to go into Crestwood. With my electronic metal detector, we should have no trouble locating the professor's creel. I'll have several hours' work on it, but by the time your father is ready to return, I should have it in top working shape."

"And what am I supposed to be doing while you're working in the Crime Lab?" I hated to ask the question, because I knew I wouldn't like the answer. Brains is always giving me the tough jobs, and sometimes they're dangerous, too. I don't mind going on dangerous assignments when Brains is with me. Most always detectives work in pairs. That's to give one another protection. But working by myself . . . that can be scary.

"You can be making a most important contribution to the case we have undertaken while I am away," Brains said. This, I knew, was the flattery gambit. Brains was buttering me up. He was just about to spread jam as well when I cut in.

"All right, Operative X," I replied, "skip the snow job and tell me what you want me to do."

Brains frowned. He clasped his hands and rubbed them together.

"It should be quite simple, Operative Three. It should, in fact, be most enjoyable."

Now I knew I was in for it.

"I want you to go to Wonder Park. That should be an assignment to gladden anyone's heart. It is my surmise that Blackie, with his show business background—working for the professor—would naturally gravitate to a similar occupation. Therefore, knowing the professor was coming to the lake, where better could he find employment and lodging, and be able to put into effect his plan to rob the professor?"

Brains can't be beaten when it comes to logic.

"All you have to do is wander around Wonder Park," Brains said, "and see if you can spot Blackie. You might even be able to get near enough to him to overhear him discussing his plans with his confederate. However, I think great care is essential to your carrying out the assignment."

Brains didn't have to tell me that! Creeps, all he was asking was for me to spy on a robber, a dangerous one who had already committed one assault and attempted another. And here I was supposed to spy on this criminal in broad daylight. And not get caught.

"Operative Three," Brains said sternly, "twice we have been close to Blackie, near the professor's cottage the night we used the flare and again when we chased his boat away from the professor on the lake. We have no idea whether he knows us by sight or not. Therefore, be on guard at all times."

"Thanks a lot, Brains," I said to myself, not out loud. He didn't have to tell me to be on guard. I didn't want to mix with Blackie.

"The park opens at noon, as you know," Brains continued. "Get there early. Mingle with the crowds. Then, once you have completed your mission, stop off at the professor's on your way home. We must make sure he is safe."

I was also going to make good and sure that James MacDonald Carson, otherwise known as Operative Three, was also safe.

"Your father and I ought to be back at about six o'clock. You and I will rendezvous at the dock for a conference. Good luck, Operative Three."

"Have a nice quiet day in the lab, X," I said. But Brains ignored my sarcasm and joined my father.

I spent part of the morning helping Mom around the house and the rest of it spinning around the lake in the boat. Right after lunch I filled the outboard with gasoline and pointed toward Wonder Park. It took me about forty-five minutes to make the run. I beached the boat and walked up the slight rise leading·from the lake shore to the park.

There weren't too many people around this early. Cars filled with picnic-bound families were coming in all the time, though, and by two-thirty, I felt it was safe to start searching for Blackie. I just laid low until then.

To make myself as inconspicuous as possible, I joined a two-family party. Each family had so many kids— about six each—that I don't think either set of parents knew whether I was one of the other's kids or not. Anyway, I stuck with them as they roamed around the park. I got pretty sick of the merry-go-round. After the third time around, I got off and waited until the small fry took their fourth ride. Jeepers, those kids set up a howl to take a fifth ride. But their parents finally got firm enough with them to drag them away. Was I ever glad.

I tagged along as the families headed over toward a long, low row of booths. You know the kind I mean. You see them at every fair or carnival or amusement park. There's always a wheel of fortune or two, where you plunk your money down on a number and maybe win a

Kewpie Doll, and there's a shooting gallery and a dart game—things like that. We stopped at the wheel of fortune first. I even played a few numbers myself. I didn't win anything.

From the take-a-chance-and-win-a-beautiful-expensive-doll booth, we moved along to where you buy three balls for a quarter and heave them at three wooden bottles mounted as a triangle. And there was Blackie. He was running the booth. His heavy brows and mean face didn't look any more pleasant in the daylight than they did by the light of a flaring book of matches in the dark woods.

"Step right up, folks," he was chanting. "Three balls for the fourth part of a dollar. Only twenty-five cents. Knock down the three bottles and take your pick of valuable prizes."

Blackie kept repeating these words in a sing-song voice. He never smiled once. In fact, he looked as if he wanted to bite the kids. I looked at the valuable prizes. There wasn't one in the whole lot that you couldn't buy in the Crestwood Variety Store for fifteen cents. But, I shouldn't be too critical. The two papas had a great time heaving those balls. I bet they both had sore arms the next day.

I stayed around Wonder Park until four-thirty. I kept as close to Blackie's booth as I could, without being too conspicuous. I didn't want someone getting suspicious of my hanging around. Blackie stayed right on the job all the time. He didn't confer with anyone. I felt my afternoon was wasted. I hadn't detected a thing. All I had done was prove Brains was right—that Blackie had taken a job at the park.

I was kind of discouraged as I headed back up the lake toward the professor's cottage.

A lot I'd have to report to Brains!

But it turned out I did. What I found out at the professor's house was important, very important. We really had a crime on our hands now. I could hardly wait for my rendezvous with my partner.

Chapter 9

The Professor Disappears

Brains, Mom and Dad were already at the supper table when I came in bursting with excitement at what I had discovered at the cottage, "By Itself." I didn't get a chance to say anything, though.

"You are late, James. You know how I dislike your being late for meals," my father said.

"Yes sir. I'm sorry, Dad," I said, bottling my news. I was hoping he wasn't too angry. If he were, then he might make me go to my room right after supper. And I had things to tell Brains, and things to do with him.

"Well, just see that it doesn't happen again. Vacation or not, you're to be on time for meals."

Dad must have had a good round of golf for him to let me off that easy. Mom knew I was all wound up. She could tell, I guess, from the way I kept looking at Brains, and trying to convey the fact that I had big news by making funny expressions.

"Eat more slowly, son," Mom said. I was racing through my supper as if there was no tomorrow.

"May I be excused now?" I asked, folding up my napkin.

"No pie, Jimmy? I baked a fresh blueberry today."

Home-made blueberry pie is one of my special favorites. Although I could hardly hold myself in, I had to have a piece of that pie. I also knew that if I didn't, Mom would surely know something was up. She was a quiz expert when she thought something was in the wind, and I couldn't answer her questions now. So, I whomped through a large hunk of pie.

Pheww! I thought supper would never be over. And it wasn't. My father was in a top mood. His putts must have been super and his tee shots duper. He wanted to talk.

"That is a most interesting device you have put together, Brains," he said. He leaned back in his chair and took out his pipe. This was going to take time. The pipe told me that. And time was what I didn't have much of. It was essential that the firm of Benton and Carson go into immediate action.

"Thanks, Mr. Carson," Brains said, pleased as he could be. Of course, he didn't know what I had to tell him, so he was only too happy to sit back and yak with Dad.

"I remember seeing land mine detectors being used in training during the last war," Dad went on. "I never used one myself. But my battalion went out to a simulated mine field and observed while the men in the detonation units demonstrated them. Is your device on the same general principle, Brains?"

"Yes sir. I have an army manual on land mines, their detection and destruction. The land mine detector works by locating buried metal."

"And it will be just as effective under water?"

"Oh, yes sir. I checked that out with one of the members of the science department at Crestwood college."

"Well, maybe you'll find some sunken treasure," Dad said, beaming.

My heart leaped into my throat. Did Dad know what we were up to? Had Brains let something slip about it on the trip to town and back? No, he couldn't have. Brains wouldn't do that. But I sure wanted to hear him tell me so himself.

Finally the talk was over. Dad got up, stretched, and went out on the front porch. I fairly leaped through the kitchen out to the back porch. Brains followed at a more leisurely pace.

"I detect, Operative Three," he said on joining me, "that you have something of major interest to impart."

"You just bet I have, Operative X. I've really got news for you. The professor is gone!"

I waited for that bombshell to rock my partner and it did. He grabbed me by the arm and we hurried down to the dock.

"Fill me in, Operative Three. Don't spare a single detail."

"Well, when I got to the professor's. . . ."

"From the beginning, Operative Three. Start with your trip to Wonder Park."

I gave that to him fast. I told him about spotting Blackie.

"Just as I had figured," he said, pleased with himself. "Now, the professor is missing, you say?"

"I sure do. And I think disappearance is due to foul play."

"Proceed."

"I got to the professor's cottage just after five o'clock. I suspected something was wrong as I walked up the path. The animals were setting up a terrific uproar. It sounded like the jungle in a Tarzan picture."

"There was no sign of the professor?"

I shook my head. "No. I called out for him. No answer. I went up to the cottage and knocked, back and front doors. No answer."

"You didn't go in?" Brains asked.

"I didn't have to," I replied with a snap. "No answer, no professor. And those animals were whooping it up . . ." Brains cut me off.

"Not an entirely wise deduction, Operative Three. Until we inspect the premises, we can't be certain the professor is gone."

"I felt it in my bones, Operative X."

"A hardly scientific approach toward ascertaining a person's disappearance," Brains came back sharply. "We must get over to the professor's cottage at once. Let's move."

I ran back up to our cottage to tell Mom we were going out for a boat ride, and we were soon speeding down the lake. When we were getting near the cottage, I felt Brains' hand on my arm.

"Cut the motor," he hissed in my ear. I did.

We rowed the rest of the way, making as little noise as we could. We beached the boat just this side of the professor's dock, and once again we were creeping through the woods. I didn't like it tonight any better than I did the other night.

"They may still have the professor in their power," Brains said. "They may be torturing him to extract the whereabouts of the money creel."

I gulped. I surely hoped not. That would be a rotten thing to do to a kindly old man who loved animals.

Suddenly I froze. Brains stopped stock-still, too. There was a loud rustling in a low bush right in front of us. We stood there, our hearts pounding.

We heard a sudden scurrying, and out of that bush came an animal as big as a lion. Well, as big as an alley cat, anyway. It came barreling along right at us. It hit Brains on one leg, careened off and struck my right ankle, then fled toward the lake.

When our nerves calmed down, and we were breathing steadily but hurriedly, we realized what it was. A big water rat! Those I definitely don't care for.

We moved forward again, creeping nearer and nearer the cottage. Why we were so careful, I can't tell you now. I guess it's because we're always cautious and quiet when we're casing a situation. But we needn't have been. Those animals were still setting up a clatter that would have frightened a safari on a big game hunt in darkest Africa.

"There's no light in the cottage, Operative X," I observed as we reached the clearing around the cottage. It was a silly thing to say. Brains could see that as well as I could.

Brains led the way. We still moved as stealthily as we could, particularly as we mounted the three steps leading to the porch. Blackie and his confederate could be inside, watching our approach in the moonlight. They'd jump us for sure.

Brains reached for the doorknob. There was no point in knocking. If the professor was inside, he was being held prisoner. He would never let his animals become as frantic as they were.

My partner carefully turned the doorknob. The door wasn't locked.

"Operative Three," he whispered. "Be ready to attack. I'm going to throw this door open, and we'll charge in."

Oh boy, I thought to myself, this could be it!

Brains threw the door open. We charged. An object came hurtling through the door. It struck me bang in the face. I toppled over backward and fell in a heap on the porch.

"Help, Brains! Help! They've got me."

I just lay there for a few moments. Nothing more happened. I started to say something to Brains and found I had a hard time talking because my mouth was full of feathers. Then I heard Brains chuckling softly. I didn't like that.

The light went on. Brains stood silhouetted in the doorway looking down at me. My hand went to my mouth. I plucked out three black feathers. Suddenly, from out by the trailer-zoo came a high, raspy imitation of the professor's voice, joining with the clamor of the animals. "Rawwk! 'Ot's goot! 'Ot's goot!" It was Edgar Allan Crow.

I knew what had happened then. Good old Eddie the

Crow must have been closed inside the room. When Brains threw the door open, the crow had come streaking out with jet speed into the face of a private detective named Jimmy Carson.

I got up. I was furious. "If you think it's funny, Barclay Benton, to get smacked in the face by a crow, then I'd just like to see it happen to you sometime."

"And when it does, Operative Three, you have my full permission to laugh at me. You must admit there is humor in the situation."

My sense of humor came back as the shock of being bird-strafed wore off. I started chuckling too. "Okay, Operative X. I guess it was pretty funny."

There was nothing funny inside the house, though. A cyclone tearing through the house could hardly have done any more damage. The living room, both bedrooms and the kitchen had been torn apart. The professor's clothes were strewn all over the floor. Bureau drawers had been pulled out and tossed about. The mattress had been ripped off the bed. A sheet dangled over the overhead light. Everywhere we looked our eyes met evidence that someone had made a thorough, wild search of that cottage. They hadn't cared how much damage they did in their hunt.

"They've been here all right, Operative Three," Brains said. I could have said "you can say that again," but I knew how much Brains hated clichés.

"They were probably here when you visited the cottage earlier," Brains continued.

"How could they have been?" I demanded. "Blackie was still at the park when I left."

"Are you positive he didn't recognize you?"

I pondered this question a moment. I couldn't be positive, of course, although I didn't think he had.

"Had he spotted you, he could very well have thought you were checking as to his whereabouts. Obviously, Blackie would not want to be pin-pointed. He may think the professor sent you to track him down and report him to the authorities."

That might sound like wild thinking to some people. Not to me though. I'd known Brains to hit the nail on the head too many times to start trying to explode his theories.

"But Operative X, if that is the case, how could he have gotten here before I did?"

"Elementary," he replied in his best Sherlock Holmes manner. "You came by boat. He came by car. The road is a direct route to the cottage. By boat you have to come around Knob Point. And the boat is slower, too."

He was right again.

There wasn't any point in hanging around the cottage any longer. The damage had been done. The interior of the cottage had been ripped apart. The professor was gone. Our only satisfaction lay in the fact that the crooks hadn't gotten the money. It was safe. Yeah, safe, but in a pretty sorry spot.

We turned out the lights and went out to the trailer-zoo. My assailant, Edgar Allan Crow, was perched on the roof. He stared down angrily at the beam of our flashlight, as if to say, "Give me back my feathers."

I opened the door of the trailer. Eddie Crow flew right in and squatted down on his nest. The noise the other animals were making was still deafening.

"They're hungry. It's far past their feeding time," Brains said. "You left the park at five. That's about the time the professor gives his animals their night feeding. I shouldn't be surprised if Blackie and his aide jumped the professor as he was feeding them."

We looked around a bit. There were signs the trailer and the car had been thoroughly searched. We went back to the trailer and fed the animals.

"Only one animal missing," Brains reported.

"Which one, Operative X."

"Xenophon, the waltzing mouse. He rides in the car with the professor. You noticed, I trust, that the glove compartment has a screened, instead of a solid, door. That's Xenophon's place of honor. He's not there, so he must have been in the professor's pocket when he was taken away."

The animals had quieted down. Their stomachs were filled. They were settling themselves for the night.

"Let's go, Operative X," I said. "Nothing more we can do here tonight."

"Yes, you're right. We can't pursue our search for the professor. That we must undertake at the first signs of dawn tomorrow." He paused. "I am concerned about the animals. Perhaps one of us should stay here the rest of the night with them. Care for a job of animal-sitting, Operative Three?"

"What," I howled. "Spend the night in a lonely cabin in the middle of the woods with a bunch of crazed animals!" I was really sore about such a suggestion. Then I heard Brains chuckle again. He was pulling my leg.

"Come on," I said, and charged off angrily toward the boat.

If I hadn't been so burned up at Brains, maybe we could have caught one of the crooks right then and there. But I plunged down the path like a bull elephant charging through a cane brake, and making just as much noise. I looked up from the path just in time to see a figure leap out of our boat, dash up the beach and disappear into the woods.

"Brains," I shouted, and took off after the figure. I didn't stop to think. I was still in too furious a mood. I must have gone a hundred feet into the deep, dark woods until my better senses took over. I called off my one-man chase and went back to the boat.

Brains greeted me with: "He's been here, too."

The two seat cushions in the boat had been slit open.
The storage well up forward where we kept the fishing
gear had been thoroughly searched.

We knew definitely now that Blackie and his confederate knew our boat was the one that had scared them
off the day they'd attacked the professor in mid-lake.

There were no two ways about it. We had become
deeply involved.

Chapter 10

Found or Lost?

"One conclusion becomes inescapable from today's events," Brains said as we headed up the lake to our cottage.

"And that is?" I asked.

"Blackie and his confederates have spotted us. They know that we are working with the professor to defy them."

Well, that conclusion seemed obvious, even to me. I wondered, though, whether they had spotted me and Brains or just me. Blackie could have seen me hanging around at Wonder Park. But it seemed more likely that we had been spotted the first time we had a run in with them when they attacked the professor's boat on the lake.

I had good reason to think this. You see, I don't stand out in a crowd, not like Brains does. I look pretty much like any other boy my age, right height, right weight. I've got dark brown hair, same color eyes, a little darker than my hair, maybe. My round face has a sprinkling of freckles. About the only thing that's unusual about me is my double-jointed left thumb. I doubt that *it* could have been noticed across the distance of water that separated us that day.

But Brains is something else again. I've told you he had hair the color of a fresh carrot. He's tall, skinny, has a long, bony nose, and he wears glasses. People turn to look at him when he walks by.

So, if either of us had been identified by Blackie, it sure must have been Brains. Brains and our boat. Oh, sure, they could have spotted me, too—just from being with Brains.

"Which means," Brains continued, "that we must be more than ever on the alert. We must guard our every movement. Blackie must think we have the money, or know where it is. Otherwise, why would our boat cushions be slit? Money could very easily be concealed in boat cushions."

We reached our dock and secured the boat. We got ready for bed in record time. I was dog tired. Brains wanted to read a while before going to sleep, but I protested. For once, he went along with me. Guess he must have been as tired as I was.

Creeps, the dreams I had that night. Birds kept flying around me, darting at my head. A seal kept barking. And sort of in the distance, vague and shadowy, I could just make out a little white mouse doing a slow, graceful waltz.

I came out of that dream with a start. Brains came to a sitting position at the same time. Both of us just sat up in the bed for a few moments, clutching the sheet. I turned on the light and looked around for whatever it was that woke us up. Brains spotted it right away. There was a hole in the window screen big enough to put your fist through.

He was really a sight as he flapped out of bed, his bony knees showing below his short pajamas.

The noise that had awakened us was the twanging of the screen, followed by a thud. It didn't take us long to find the noise maker. A rock, the size of a billiard ball, had been hurled through our window. But the rock wasn't what got us all excited. It was the message that was tied to the rock.

Brains unfolded the paper, and we huddled under the bed light to read it. As we read, our hearts sank. All our suspicions about the professor's fate were confirmed. I'll never forget that note. It was frightening.

My good boys,

I have been kidnapped. The money they want. I am remembering you said the money you could find, so please do it soon. To my animals I must be getting back. If the money you can find, leave it in mein car where Xenophon sleeps. Then I will be free. If you tell the police, more bad things will happen to me. Feed animals please.

The note wasn't signed. It didn't have to be.

"Creeps, Brains," I said, "Isn't he a wonderful old man? Worrying about his animals. Doesn't say a thing about how he is, or what Blackie must have done to him. He really loves those animals."

"Yes, Operative Three, we must care for the animals. And we must locate the professor."

"Isn't this getting too big for us, though, Operative X? Shouldn't we call in the police?"

"You read in the note what the professor said would happen if we did," Brains replied.

"Yes, I know. But he's been kidnapped. He's in danger."

Brains was tugging at his ear lobe. Brains was thinking.

"It is my feeling, Operative Three, that we should spend all of tomorrow trying to find the professor. We should also try to find the money. Then, if we fail, we'll have to go to the police. Remember, Officer McKeon is coming back out here Thursday. We'll give ourselves thirty-six hours. Then, if we are unsuccessful, we'll tell the whole story to Officer McKeon."

A zillion questions were racing through my mind. Could we find the money? And if we did, could we trust those crooks to release the professor if we *did* give them the money? How could we work out the exchange?

Tomorrow sure looked like a big day. It was.

We were up the next morning before my Mom and Dad. We fixed ourselves a fast breakfast and headed down the lake. Brains had his underwater metal detector along. Our first idea had been to test it, have a trial run before using it to locate the creel. But we gave that idea up. We didn't have the time. And time was the important factor now. We were worried about the professor's safety. Each hour that went by meant he was in more and more danger.

We rounded Knob Point and reached the spot where the professor thought he had dropped the creel overboard.

"We'll start here, Operative Three," Brains said. "You row the boat. We'll want to go even slower than we can with the motor throttled to trolling speed."

"Why do I have to do the rowing? You know how," I protested.

"My entire attention must be devoted to the detector," Brains replied.

He had me. Once again, good old Operative Three was in for the hard part of the job.

"Of course," Brains continued, "when we locate any metal, then you will have the fun of diving for it."

I brightened up at that. Creeps, what a thrill it would be to find that metal creel.

Brains dropped the long wire lead of the detector overboard. One end was attached to the oblong-shaped box containing the batteries and the dial indicator. The other end of the wire had a microphone-shaped disc attached to it. When the disc plinked against the bottom, Brains nodded his head and I bent my back to the oars, pulling gently.

"Line the boat up between a tree to the stern and a tree directly ahead of the bow. Then try to hold as direct a course as you can," Brains said. "We will criss-cross this area leaving about eight feet between each course. This detector should pick up any metal for four feet on each side."

I rowed about a hundred feet, keeping that boat on as true a course as if I were the navigator on a Polaris submarine. Nothing. Not once did the dial on the detector swing. Not a peep from the buzzer which would sound if we contacted metal. Brains was all attention. He had headphones on. These, he explained to me, were even more sensitive than the dial. He had it worked out all right. He always did.

On our first return, we struck oil. I mean, the detector picked up its first metal object.

Brains straightened up, his face all smiles.

"Over you go, Operative Three. This could be it."

I hurled the anchor overboard, and quickly put on the skin diving suit. Down I went. I followed the lead line down to a bottom of pure white sand. Near the bottom a sunfish swam up to me and looked me right in the eye through my face mask. It reached out and touched it. It sped away.

Once on bottom, I cleared my face mask because some water had seeped in, and started looking around. I swam in a circle around the metal detecting disc. I saw nothing that looked like the professor's creel. What, I asked myself, was the metal that had activated the detector? Then I saw it. A horseshoe, of all things.

I picked up the horseshoe and shot to the surface, holding the horseshoe over my head.

I took off my face mask and grinned at Brains. He didn't smile back. There was a look of disappointment on his face.

"How ever in the world did a horseshoe get out here in the middle of the lake?" he asked.

"You've heard of sea horses, haven't you?" I cracked, making what I thought was a funny. No smile from my partner though.

"This is no time for levity, Operative Three."

I climbed back in the boat and we resumed our search. I went up and down like an elevator five times in the next half an hour. That bottom seemed to be littered with metal. And what a haul I made. One rusty motor-oil can, a fluke off an old anchor, a toy wind-up boat some kid had scuttled, and the darndest thing—an alarm clock. I guess some vacationer made really sure he wasn't going to have to get up early in the morning. He must have had a great pitching arm to wing the alarm this far out in the lake.

We kept probing and diving for another hour. By that time the bottom of our boat looked like a junk yard.

"Let's take a break, Operative X," I said. "I'm tired." All that diving and rowing was fun, but it was tiring, too.

For a while we just drifted. There was hardly any breeze that morning. The boat barely moved. I sat there enjoying the sun and thinking that we had a much bigger job than we ever expected. Brains must have felt the same way.

"We must persevere, Operative Three. True, there are many more metal objects on the bottom than I expected to find. But I feel certain we shall locate the creel."

I shrugged my shoulders. Just then, Brains' detector buzzed.

"Ready to try again, Operative Three?"

"Sure, why not," I replied. But I guess I was losing interest because I didn't look forward to another dunk. I was beginning to feel like a submarine on a trial run. But down I went anyhow. The bottom was a little muddier at this spot. I couldn't see very well. I swam around, feeling with my hands and feet. My left foot touched something and I craw-fished backward.

"Eureka!" I shouted, and got a mouthful of water as a result. But I had found it! I found the creel! Boy, I surfaced fast—much faster than Officer McKeon had said a diver should surface. In my excitement, I forgot all about his instructions.

I bobbed above the water, holding the creel over my head triumphantly.

"Got it, Brains! I got it!"

Brains was as excited as I was. He started dancing up and down, but stopped quickly. He was rocking the boat.

In my delight, I straightened out on my back, floating, and clutching the creel to my chest. Boy, did I ever feel great.

"Bring it in, Operative Three," Brains called. I kicked and edged back to the boat. I was just about to hand the creel to Brains when we heard it. We heard the sound of another boat. Its motor was revving up to full throttle. I swirled around in the water in the direction Brains was looking. His face had become clouded with worry. My diving mask was covered with drops of water, so I couldn't see what was upsetting him. Quickly, I shoved the mask up on my forehead.

Creeps!

Blackie, in the speedboat, was barrelling toward us like a barracuda.

Chapter 11

Blackie Threatens

"What will I do with this thing? What will I do with it?" I shouted frantically.

"Drop it!" Brains shouted back.

I did. Down it went. Once more the professor's creel, filled with money, sank to the bottom. My heart sank along with it. Creeps, here we'd found the money, and now we'd lost it again.

Blackie's speedboat was aiming straight at us. I thought he was going to ram our boat. But, at the last moment, he swerved, throwing up a wake that nearly swamped our smaller boat. It also washed over my head, making me gasp for breath.

When I got the water out of my mouth, eyes and lungs, I spotted Brains holding onto the gunwale of our boat. He let go with one hand and motioned me to the boat. I swam over.

"We have to act fast, Operative Three," he said. "But it is important that we remain calm as we do so."

Now just how can you act fast and be calm at the same time, I wondered? Brains went on.

"We mustn't let Blackie get the idea that we have located the creel. If he does, there's no reason why he can't get skin diving equipment, too, and search this spot."

"So what can we do?"

Brains thought about this for a few seconds. "Make another dive. Right at this spot . . ."

"What?" I interrupted. "Right where the creel is? That will be a dead give away."

"On the contrary, Operative Three. You dive here, yes. But you don't bring anything up. Unless you find some other piece of junk metal. If you can, that will be great."

A bubble of what Brains was thinking started ballooning in my mind. Blackie had stopped his boat about a hundred feet from us. He cut the motor. There was no doubt he was going to watch our operation. He knew we must be diving for the creel. The professor must have told him.

"When you go down this time, Operative Three," Brains said, "stay down several minutes. When you come up, we'll move from this spot. Oh, don't worry, I have this position carefully plotted. I have pin-pointed it by means of reference points on the shore. I feel positive that we can relocate this spot quickly."

That was good enough for me. If Brains said so, it was just as good as marking the spot with a big liquid X. Down I went again. When I reached bottom, I just sat there, I sat there until I had counted to two hundred, and I counted slowly, too. I couldn't see the creel, but I knew Brains' gadget could pick it out when the time came. I did find another metal object—a piggy bank, of all things, I couldn't figure how it got there even with my wildest guesses. Kind of funny though. Here Blackie was waiting for us to bring up a creel full of money, and I was going to surface with an empty piggy bank. Oh, it was empty, all right. I shook it against my ear.

When I surfaced, I shook my head at Brains in an exaggerated NO. I could see Blackie and his pal craning their necks to see if I had come up with the creel. I tossed the piggy bank into the boat.

"Stay in the water this time, Operative Three," Brains said, "and hang on to the stern. I'll tow us to another spot."

I hung on and Brains rowed about twenty-five feet. I dove again. We repeated this process several times, each time moving ten or twenty feet farther away from the spot where the creel lay on the lake's bottom.

Blackie moved each time we did—always keeping our operation under close observation.

"I'm running out of air, Operative X," I told Brains. "One more dive, and we've had it."

Brains nodded his head, and down I went again. I didn't stay long this time. When I surfaced, I climbed into the boat, and took off the diving equipment. Brains started our motor. Blackie started the engine of the speedboat. He headed toward us. He swerved toward us, but not to do any damage.

"Find that money in a hurry," he shouted as he sped by, "if you ever want to see the old man again."

Creeps, we were getting into it deeper and deeper.

We watched the speedboat disappear in the direction of Wonder Park. I looked at my partner.

"What do we do now, Operative X? Go back and get the money?"

"Oh, no, Operative Three. Blackie's withdrawal may be a ruse. A ruse intended to make us think he had departed so we might start diving again. He may have seen you when you surfaced with the creel."

I hadn't thought of that angle. Brains, though, doesn't miss a trick.

"Well, since you're sure where the creel is, I'm just as happy that you don't want to get it now. I'd have to dive on the emergency air supply, and that isn't safe."

So we headed for home. On the way, Brains summed up our position.

"The picture has become clear, Operative Three," he said. "We know these positive facts: one, that Blackie is holding the professor prisoner; two, we know where the money is and we can get it at any time; three, well . . ."

"Sure, we know one and two, but just what about three?"

Tugging at his ear lobe, Brains answered slowly. "Three is how do we safely effect the professor's release? Can we trust Blackie to free the professor if we give him the money?"

"Not to give you a short answer, Operative X," I said, "but the reply to your query is 'no.'"

"I agree. Thus, even though we are the catalyst for the professor's release . . ."

"The 'cat-what?'" I cut in.

"The agent—in this case agents—by which our actions bring about a further action—the release of the professor."

Well, I guess I got it. But Brains could have told me about it in simpler words.

"The plan I have in mind is this: we will leave a note in Xenophon's nest. Blackie will be checking it regularly for the money. The note will direct Blackie to meet us off Knob Point *with* the professor. In this way, we will be certain the professor is free and unharmed before we even reveal where the money is."

"And once we have the professor in our boat, then I dive for the creel and turn it over to Blackie."

"You have grasped the idea with the keenness of mind that makes you such a valuable member of the firm of Benton and Carson," Brains said. "The solution to our dilemma has become simple."

I was flattered by that "keenness of mind" statement, all right, but I wasn't so sure about how simple it was going to be. In fact, further complications developed that very night.

Chapter 12

Mystery Blonde

Right after supper that evening, when the sun was beginning to set over the western edge of the lake, Brains and I headed back to the professor's cottage. We had to feed the animals.

Were they ever glad to see us! Either that, or they were mighty hungry. They set up a howl when we approached, then calmed down again as we gave them their food.

We were both in the trailer-zoo, finishing up the feeding job, when we heard someone approaching. We ducked down by Oscar, the seal's, tank. We could hear voices. They were coming closer to the trailer.

Brains crept over to the small barred window on the side the voices were coming from. He raised his head very cautiously. Then he ducked it down quickly.

"It's Blackie," he whispered to me. "And he has a young girl with him."

I crept over and took a quick look. Blackie and this girl were standing about ten feet away from the trailer, talking as casually as if all was right with the world. The girl was very pretty. She was a blonde, and it was still just light enough for me to see she had honey-colored hair, cut kind of short. She looked about my sister Ann's age. I strained my ears to overhear what they were saying.

"Here they are! Here they are!"

I jumped back, feeling like a dagger had been stuck in my back. Brains had already scrambled under Oscar's tank. I jammed myself in beside him. We both knew we were goners. The conversation outside had stopped. A light, musical laugh broke the tension.

"That must be Edgar Allan Crow," the girl said. "Doesn't he sound almost human?" Talk about being relieved! I sighed like a locomotive letting off steam in a railroad yard. I looked at Brains and in the fading daylight, I could see a nervous smile flickering across his face.

"More! More! More! Rawwk!"

It was Edgar jabbering again.

Brains and I remained under the water tank. We didn't know whether Blackie and the girl were going to come into the trailer-zoo or not.

"The animals are quiet," we heard the girl say, "all except Edgar. Has someone been feeding and taking care of them?"

"Yeah, they're being looked after," Blackie said. I knew that he knew who was looking after the animals— us, Brains and I. Then we heard the most puzzling conversation.

"You're positive he's safe?" the girl asked.

"You can bet all the dollars you're going to get on that, Gretchen," Blackie replied.

I could feel Brains' bony hand clutch my arm. He was thinking the same thing I was. What dollars was Blackie referring to? The professor's?

"I was worried that something might have gone wrong," Gretchen said.

"What could go wrong? Chick's with him," Blackie asked in reply.

"Oh, I suppose I'm worrying about nothing," Gretchen said. "But he is an old man. And he's not as strong as he once was."

I could follow her trend of thought. An old man held in captivity could get sick, could have a heart attack or something.

"Well you just don't worry your pretty head about

the professor," Blackie said. "Everything's under control. Will we get together tomorrow night?"

"All right," Gretchen replied. "I'll come over to Wonder Park as soon after eight as I can make it."

The couple walked away. We crawled out from under Oscar's tank and peeked out the window. We could just see them heading toward the dock. We waited until we heard the engine of the speedboat start.

"Come on, Operative Three," Brains said. "We've got to see which way they're heading."

We ran down to the dock. We could still see the white wake made by the speedboat. It was heading across the lake in the direction of Community Camp where Ann was a counselor.

"We'll follow them," Brains said.

I didn't stop to ask any questions. We headed across the lake, too.

The speedboat was much faster than our small craft. We were lucky, though. We got across the lake just in time to see the speedboat leaving the shore of the cove just opposite Community Camp. There was another girls' camp there—called Camp Sandy Cove, natch.

"We can head back home now, Operative Three. We have learned where this girl is from. Obviously, she must be a counselor at Camp Sandy Cove."

"Oh, sure, we know that. But who is she? Do you think she's in with Blackie?"

"From her conversation with Blackie, such would seem to be indicated," Brains replied.

"But she's such a nice-looking girl," I protested. "She looks sort of like my sister Ann. I mean, the same kind of a girl, cleancut and stuff, like those counselors always are."

"Appearances, Operative Three, can often be deceiving."

I shook my head. I just couldn't believe it. I couldn't believe a nice-looking girl like that Gretchen could be in on a kidnapping with a guy like Blackie.

"We must find out more about this girl, Operative Three," Brains said. "She could be the key to the whole mystery."

How right Brains was, although we didn't know it at the time.

The next morning we set out to find out more about Gretchen. We took the boat across the lake and cruised around Sandy Cove. There was a swim meet going on between Camp Sandy Cove and Community Camp. I could see Ann with a group of small fry.

It was also easy to pick out Gretchen because of her light hair shining almost like aluminum when the sun struck it.

We stayed outside the roped-in swimming area where the races were taking place. A group of girl kids, maybe ten or eleven years old, were being mother-henned by

Gretchen. Four of them lined up with four girls the same size from Community Camp. The start and finishing markers were about twenty yards apart. At a signal, the eight minnows started swimming like crazy, making more splash than progress.

Camp Sandy Cove won. The winning team pranced out of the water and surrounded Gretchen. They raised their squeaky little voices into a cheer. It went:

> "Gretchen! Gretchen!
> Veeeee-Emmmmm Rand!
> She's our coach
> And she is grand!"

So now we knew her name.

"Gretchen Rand," Brains said, half aloud.

"That's her name all right. And those kids think she's really something. Now how could a girl like that be mixed up in a kidnapping?" I asked.

Brains wasn't listening, wasn't paying any attention to what I said.

"Gretchen Rand," he repeated the name. "But I don't understand one part of that cheer."

"What part? Her name's plain enough."

"Oh yes. I am fully aware of that, Operative Three. What puzzles me is that part of the cheer that went Veeee-Emmmmm?"

"So what of it?" I asked. "Probably just stands for something dumb like 'very' and er, well, 'magnificent' maybe. Girls are always exaggerating."

Brains frowned. "I feel there is more significance to it than that, Operative Three."

Now I couldn't see anything so important about that "Veeee-Emmmmm" stuff. Brains, when he is working on a mystery, considers every little, pick-y thing.

We spent the rest of the day cruising the lake shore, looking for the professor. We inspected abandoned boat houses, peered in the windows of unrented cottages, and cottages in such bad shape nobody would rent them. We must have looked through twenty-five places. No sign of the professor. Not one tiny clue.

Along about supper time, we gave up our search. Right after supper, we set out for Wonder Park. We were going to be on the spot when Gretchen met Blackie.

Chapter 13

The Mouse Waltz

It was still daylight when we untied the mooring rope, cranked up the outboard and headed for Wonder Park. A soft, warm breeze rippled the lake's blue waters. You couldn't ask for a nicer July evening.

We took it easy on the run down the lake. It would take nearly an hour to make it, at the speed we chose, but we had plenty of time. We didn't want to get there too much before Gretchen did. We knew we couldn't take any chances on being spotted by Blackie.

When we were still a mile away from the park, we could hear the tinny sound of the merry-go-round's mechanical music. The ferris wheel was already lighted and we could see the top half of it turning lazily in the dusk.

"We must carry out this reconnaissance with the greatest of caution, Operative Three," Brains said. "Therefore, I feel it unwise for us to land at the park's dock."

"Right, Operative X. I feel the same. I'll select a secluded spot just this side of the park and we'll beach the boat there."

"Good. Somewhere between where the professor was first attacked and the park itself."

I found the ideal place. It was a small finger of an inlet, leading to a brook. The low brush and blueberry bushes came right down to the shore line. We pulled the boat up on the narrow strip of beach so that it blended with the brush in the background and would be difficult to see from the roadside.

"Lead on, Operative Three. To where do we proceed?"

"We'll cut around to the rear of the park. There are a bunch of barracks there where the park workers sleep."

It took us about ten minutes to reach the barracks. We stayed on the fringe of the woods but had a good vantage point. We could see the whole area clearly. Naked lights hanging from slender poles made our view even better.

It was ten minutes of eight when we took up our position. We waited. Except for the mosquitoes which thought Brains and I were an ideal before-bedtime snack, we were quite comfortable.

"Look! Over there," Brains whispered.

It was exactly eight o'clock.

I looked and saw Gretchen come hurrying from the amusement section of the park into the employees' quarters. We saw her stop and speak to a man. He pointed to one of the barracks.

"That must be where Blackie lives," I whispered.

Brains kept his eyes glued on Gretchen.

Gretchen nodded her head "thanks" to the man and headed for the barracks. She climbed the rickety steps to the porch and knocked on the door.

She waited. So did we.

Gretchen knocked again. After a shorter wait this time, she repeated her knock. Obviously, Blackie wasn't in. Gretchen came off the porch and headed back in the direction she had come from. We followed her, keeping a safe distance behind.

She pressed her way through the growing crowds. On a night like tonight, Wonder Park was going to have plenty of people. It made it easier for us to keep her in sight without attracting attention to ourselves.

We saw her make another inquiry. From her change in direction, I knew where she was going.

"Change of plans, Operative X," I said. "I know where she's heading. Blackie must be on duty tonight.

He works the concession where you heave three balls at some blocks of wood. Instead of following Gretchen right up to the front of the booth, let's slip around behind, and come up on one side of it."

Brains agreed with my plan. I remembered there was a narrow opening, like an alley, between Blackie's booth and the tent which housed the next row of booths. We slipped around the back of the booths. Once I tripped over a guy rope at the rear of the booth.

"Careful," cautioned Brains.

Very quietly we crept up between the two tents. Brains was in the lead. He poked his prying head a few inches beyond the front edge of the tent and drew his head back quickly.

"She's there, Operative Three." I could hear the excitement in his voice.

We had to wait. A father and his young son were tossing balls at the blocks. Blackie was chanting his come-on song.

"Hya are, folks. Three balls for a quarter. Step right up, folks, step right up. Win a valuable prize."

The boy and his father had had enough, and for the next few minutes, there was a lull at Blackie's stand. Brains and I pressed our ears to the side of the canvas. What we heard didn't explain Gretchen's part of the kidnap setup. I mean, it sure didn't make her look innocent. I felt from what we heard she was in deep.

"You've heard, then," Gretchen said.

"Oh, sure, Gretchen. You've got to stop worrying."

"Nothing's happened? Nothing's gone wrong?" Gretchen asked, and her voice sounded tense and nervous to me.

"Nope. Chick still has the professor in Middlebury. They'll be back tonight. I don't know how late, but you'd better not wait around. It will probably be after we close before Chick brings him back."

"All right, Blackie."

"You run along now. I'll see you tomorrow and you'll see that everything's in great shape."

Gretchen walked away. We saw her pass the opening slit we were using for our place of concealment. I looked up just then and grabbed Brains by the arm. A broad-shouldered man was standing glaring at us. His hands were on his hips. His eyes glowered at us. He was one of the park guards.

"Hey! You kids! What are you hiding back there for?"

This was no time for polite conversation, so we didn't answer the guard. We just turned and ran back out of that alley as fast as our legs could carry us. I headed toward the woods, thinking we'd better get to our boat and take off—but quick. Not Brains, though.

"Hold it, Operative Three," he shouted from behind me. "Where do you think you're going?"

"Anywhere but here," I shouted back. I reached the

edge of the woods and waited for Brains to catch up.

"We can't leave now, Operative Three. There is much more for us to learn."

"What more can there be? We know for sure now, don't we, that Gretchen's in on this deal. I hate to admit it. And the professor's being held in Middlebury."

Brains did a turn-about on me.

"I'm not so sure, Operative Three. Perhaps she isn't."

"What! You heard their conversation."

"True. The outward evidence seems to point to Gretchen's being part of the plot. But I thought I detected a note of real concern for the professor's safety in the girl's voice," Brains said.

"What you detected was her worrying about whether anything had slipped up. She wasn't worried about the professor's safety. And what about that Middlebury stuff? Here we spent most of yesterday searching the lake front, and all the time the professor's in Middlebury."

"I wonder about that," Brains said. "It seems highly unlikely." He paused. "Perhaps we can find out."

"Just how?" I wanted to know.

"We'll go back to the barracks Blackie occupies. Perhaps we can pick up a clue."

I didn't want to go back there any more than I wanted to take a math exam. I still hadn't forgotten that burly, broad-shouldered guard staring at me. What if he caught us snooping around again? I trailed after Brains.

We really slunk through those quarters, trying to keep in the shadows, our heads swiveling from side to side to see if anyone was watching us.

I stood guard by the steps as Brains mounted the porch of Blackie's end of the barracks. A card on the door said, "Blackstone." Brains peeked through the window. He didn't stay there long.

"Too dark to see anything, Operative Three," he said when he re-joined me. "I noticed that the rear of the shack seems to be better lighted. Probably from one of the pole lights shining in from the rear. We'll try it from back there."

Here we go again, I thought, as we slipped around to the rear of the shack. Sure enough, the light did shine through the rear window so you could see pretty well into the room. Brains looked. I looked.

"You see anything, Operative X?" I asked.

Brains shook his head.

"Let's get out of here then," I urged.

Brains just stood there. It was quiet behind the barracks. There were just the usual nighttime woods sounds and, coming from the brightly lighted midway beyond a grove of trees, the music of the merry-go-round. Then I realized that Brains was humming. Humming! At a time like this? I stepped up beside him at the window. He was staring at something on the window sill, just inside the screen. I bent my head closer and looked.

Brains was humming in time with the merry-go-round music, and there on the window sill, waltzing in perfect time with both, was a tiny white mouse.

"It's Xenophon!" Brains said. He couldn't keep his voice low, he was so excited. I felt sure someone must have heard him. My imagination had my nerves edgier than a safety-razor blade.

Brains raised the screen window a few inches and held out his hand. Xenophon hopped happily into it.

"This proves it," Brains said.

"Proves what?" I asked.

"The professor has been held prisoner here in Blackie's quarters. Xenophon's presence could scarcely be accounted for otherwise," Brains continued. "My hunch is that the professor has recently been moved," he added.

"Why 'recently'?" I wanted to know.

Brains' answer gassed me. He held his cupped hand, where Xenophon nestled, under my nose.

"Smell!" he commanded.

Chapter 14

Oscar Aweigh!

"Limburger cheese!" The smell of it helped me choke back a howl.

"Your nose knows, Operative Three. I wish *we* could be as sure. I suspect, though, that Xenophon has recently been fed. While the odor of Limburger is somewhat over-powering, I do not believe that it would remain detect-able about the mouse for any prolonged stretch of time," Brains said.

"Then you think the professor was here not so long ago, Operative X?" I asked.

"We cannot be sure, of course. But, note the happy condition of the mouse. He shows no sign of hunger, no sign of alarm. His beloved master has not been gone long enough to arouse his animal forebodings."

"But why move the professor around like a checker? Why not keep him here in one hiding place?" I persisted.

Brains tapped one of his long fingers against the side of his head as if to jar loose his next thought.

"I feel that he was removed in time to prevent his discovery in these quarters, discovery by Gretchen upon her arrival here. Remember, Blackie told her the professor was in Middlebury."

"But if she is in on the kidnapping, why wouldn't Blackie want her to see the professor?" This whole deal was getting wackier. I couldn't figure it out.

"That, Operative Three, is a puzzlement. It is another facet to our growing mystery."

"I'll say it is! Here we think we've got everything figured out, and our mystery gets more mysterious."

"True, Operative Three. But that makes the mystery even more fascinating." Brains put Xenophon in his pocket. That was my cue to say "Let's get out of here."

"Not yet, Operative Three. Since Xenophon's cheese perfume convinces me that Professor Gus is somewhere in or near this park and not in Middlebury, I think we should look around for any sign of his whereabouts."

I couldn't argue Brains out of it, as badly as I wanted to. I don't like to remember the next hour. I didn't do much looking, either—for the professor, I mean. I kept an eye out for that big guard so he wouldn't bear down on us again.

It's a funny thing, too, how different an amusement park can be when you're not there for a good time. All the sounds that make you feel gay normally just added to my tenseness that night. The lights and shadows made by the whirling ferris wheel were eery pictures instead of gay patterns. Same way with the music. It all seemed off-key, off-beat and nerve-jangling.

I guess I was getting a mountain-size case of the jitters. When Brains finally decided to give up the search, my low spirits shot up higher than a jet pilot's headgear. I just wanted to get home. I wanted to get to bed and go to sleep.

I did not know at the time that my sleep was going to be rudely shattered at three o'clock in the morning.

"About what time do you think Officer McKeon will arrive tomorrow?" Brains asked as we headed for home up the lake.

"Ten or eleven o'clock, I guess. Why?" I asked in reply.

"We shall set eleven o'clock as our deadline. If we haven't located the professor by then, we must unfold the entire story to Officer McKeon."

Up to that moment, I thought I'd be happy when Brains decided to call in the police. That would mean we'd be free for real vacation activities instead of working on a case. But somehow, when Brains put the fact in cold, spoken words, my spirits dropped. I knew then that I'd be as disappointed as Brains would be if we didn't crack this case. It would be our first failure.

"Well, we've still got until eleven tomorrow," I said to Brains.

"Not much time, Operative Three," Brains replied. I could tell from his tone of voice that he was pretty unhappy about the setup.

"We can get up really early," I said, hoping to cheer my partner up. "We'll get up at six. Start right out."

Brains didn't answer, so I don't know whether I cheered him up any or not. By this time we had reached our landing. We moored the boat and walked in silence to the cottage. Mom and Dad were already in bed. They called out a "goodnight" to us, and we called one back. We made a nest for Xenophon in an empty coffee can. Then we went to bed.

I went to sleep the moment my head hit the pillow. I slept, sure, but also dreamed. For a time I whistled crazily around on a lop-sided ferris wheel. Then my dreams took on a nightmarish aspect. This great big guard I'd seen at the park was chasing me. I ran as hard as I could, but I seemed to be standing still. My feet were moving but my body wasn't. The guard grabbed me by the shoulders and started shaking me.

"I've got you. I've got you," he said in my dream.

I woke up fast and sat up.

It wasn't the guard shaking me by the shoulder. It was Brains. And the words I thought I heard the guard speaking were Brains'.

"I've got it! I've got it," Brains said.

"Got what? What have you got?" I asked. I was still a little dazed from my heavy but nightmarish sleep. "And what are you doing waking me at this time of the night?" I leaned over to the table beside our bed and looked at the luminous dial on my watch. It was three a.m.

"I've got the solution to the Veeeee-Emmmmm."

"To the what?" I didn't get it.

"To the Veeee-Emmmmm we heard when those kids cheered Gretchen. Say your first name, middle initial and last name," Brains said looking at me intently.

"Aw, come *on*," I whined. "It's three ayem, and no time for jokes."

"Say it," Brains insisted.

I felt like the world's sleepiest fool, but I did. Dutifully I chirped, "James M. D. Carson."

"Exactly, *exactly*," Brains crowed with glee. "Since your middle name is Mac Donald, you give yourself a double middle initial. Those swimmers were calling out Gretchen's middle initials—V. M. Now, what does V. M. remind you of."

I wanted to come up with a fast answer so we could get back to sleep. We were going to be up in less than three hours. But try as I could, nothing flickered into my empty brain. My head tank was dry.

"What is Professor Gus' last name, Operative Three?"

Now I began seeing a light.

"Von Maltzbenden, of course . . . you. . . . .?"

"Exactly, Operative Three. Gretchen's middle initials could well stand for Von Maltzbenden. And the feminine name 'Gretchen' is of Germanic origin. And we know the professor is German."

"But her last name is Rand," I said.

"True. Gretchen Von Maltzbenden Rand."

"If that's really her name, then she must be related to the professor."

"Correct, Operative Three."

"Creeps! That makes it even worse. Here she is, related to the professor, but involved with crooks trying to rob him. I don't get it."

"I don't either, Operative Three. Not completely."

Brains' not getting it either made me feel a little better. If he couldn't get it with that mind of his, then I couldn't blame myself too much for being dense. I slumped back down on the bed, thumped my pillow and closed my eyes. I could feel Brains settling back down, too. We were just too sleepy to stay awake any longer with that puzzler.

My alarm clock went off at exactly six. I grabbed it fast and shut it off. I didn't want to wake up Mom and Dad. We ate fast and in silence. We had five hours to crack this case. Only five hours, and we'd be at the deadline we'd set for ourselves.

"You straighten up, Operative Three. I want to leave a note for Officer McKeon."

I did as Brains ordered. I often do that. I rinsed out our cereal dishes and milk glasses and stacked them on the drain board. Brains had finished his note-writing by then.

"We'll take along the skin diving equipment," Brains said.

"But what's Officer McKeon going to do? He'll be wanting it when he gets here."

"My note to him tells him where we'll be at eleven," Brains replied.

It may have told Officer McKeon, all right, but it sure didn't tell me. I hadn't any idea of where we would be at eleven. And I couldn't figure out how Brains knew, either.

We headed first for the professor's cottage. We wanted to feed the animals.

"Look at Oscar," I said to Brains. The seal was just lying motionless in his tank, his bewhiskered snout resting on the edge. He didn't even want to eat. I tossed a herring into the tank. At first he ignored it. Finally, he slowly turned and gulped it down. There was no doubt about it. Oscar was heartsick. He missed the professor. Next to Xenophon, Oscar was the professor's favorite.

Looking at Oscar's sad expression gave me an idea.

"Say, how about taking Oscar along with us," I said to Brains. "He's so sad and all, maybe a swim would cheer him up."

"An excellent idea, Operative Three. Do you think we can induce him to come with us?"

"We can only try," I replied.

I opened the rear door of the trailer. The tank fitted right up against it. Then I dangled another herring about two feet away from Oscar's nose. He didn't budge. I waved the herring closer under his nose, and he started to take it. I stepped back. I repeated this process several times, each time taking another step backward farther away from Oscar. He finally got the idea. At my sixth trial, he flopped out of the tank and started flapping away after me. I kept about six feet between us, all the time drawing him nearer the dock. We made it.

Oscar took one plunge into the lake, then shot up and into our boat. When he got in, he stretched out and didn't move. He didn't even take the herring I'd used as bait to get him down to the lake. Just lay there, and believe you me, I can coin a new phrase from looking at Oscar—"sad as a seal."

"We've got to go to Wonder Park, Operative X," I

said, "if we're going to use the SCUBA. Need air for the tank. There's not enough left to do any diving."

"All right, Operative Three. And on our way down, we'll peek into any abandoned cottage we spot."

This we did. We looked through the windows of half a dozen cottages on the way down. Nothing. By the time we got to the park, it was nearly nine-thirty. Only one and a half hours to go.

The place where I got the compressed air was on the western edge of the park, away from the amusement center. The hose and regulator for the compressed air were outside a little shack. The air was a service the park provided, just as most gas stations provide free air for people's tires.

I filled the tank and we turned back.

We kept close to shore, our eyes searching the park for any evidence of Blackie, his pal or the professor.

An unopened amusement park at nine-thirty in the morning is a dreary sight. There was no sign of life. All the concessionaires and ride operators were still asleep. Those people work late hours so their day is turned around.

We weren't more than fifteen feet off shore, cruising very slowly. I looked at Oscar. He was just lying still. He was a sick seal.

As we neared the exit of the Tunnel of Thrills, Oscar raised his head. The exit opened into the lake. When the ride was operating, the boats carrying the thrill-seekers came out of the tunnel onto the lake, then were pulled by a cable back to the starting place up a ramp.

Oscar now had his snout in the air and was sniffing away like a hungry boy smelling a fresh cooked apple pie. We were directly opposite the exit of the tunnel now. All of a sudden, Oscar rose on his flippers, let out a couple of barks and leaped out of the boat. He split the water heading for the Tunnel. He didn't stop when he reached the opening. He sped right on in.

Chapter 15

The Tunnel of Thrills

"Hey, Oscar! Come back here!" I yelled. Oscar kept right on going. I could hear his barking echoing inside the Tunnel.

"What will we do, Brains?" In my excitement I forgot to call him by his code name.

"He's after something. We'll have to go in and get him."

"Into the tunnel! Into that spooky place! Creeps!"

"What else can we do?" my partner asked. "We can't leave a live seal roaming around an amusement park."

Brains was right, of course. I pointed the bow toward the big arched hole of the tunnel's entrance. You couldn't see very far inside. That gaping hole looked to me like the mouth of a hungry shark, waiting to eat us for breakfast.

I throttled the motor back to slow.

"Stand in the bow, Operative X," I directed Brains. "We don't know how deep the water is in the tunnel. We might get stuck."

Brains took up a Mark Twain position, watching the water's depth.

We eased into the tunnel. Boy, was it ever scary! This "Tunnel of Thrills" was built just like the ones they call the "Tunnel of Love" in some amusement parks. But this one wasn't built to encourage affection. About every twenty feet there was a diorama depicting some horrifying incident or legend. One scene showed a guillotine in position to drop on a victim's head. Another held a gigantic bat with blood red eyes and fangs. The park could call it the "Tunnel of Thrills." I called it the "Tunnel of Horrors."

We could hear Oscar barking just ahead of us. He was barking fast and frantically. We could barely see as we went after him. The only light, since the park was still closed, came from outside. And it wasn't very much.

We caught up with Oscar. He had leaped out of the water onto a narrow ledge that ran along the side of the tunnel. He was in front of a diorama showing Pocahontas stopping her father from giving the ax to John Smith.

"Come on, Oscar, get off that ledge and into the boat," I called. For an answer Oscar flounced toward the back of the diorama, knocking over Pocahontas as he went.

"Try some herring on him," Brains suggested.

I put the fish on an oar blade and stretched it toward him. But Oscar just sat there yapping away, clapping his flippers together. I tried wheedling. "Here Oscar, here. Nice piece of fish?" He stopped yapping long enough to turn his nose up at me and the whole idea.

"There's something back there he wants, Operative X," I said to Brains.

"Or someone," was Brains' excited reply.

"You mean. . . ."

Brains nodded his head. "It could be. You go back outside. Walk along the side of the tunnel until you're opposite the spot where you hear Oscar barking."

"How'm I going to do that?" I demanded. "Swim? While you stay here in the boat?"

"Use the ledge. It leads to the outside," Brains said.

I looked at that ledge. It wasn't more than eighteen inches wide. What if I slipped, and fell into that dark, cold-looking water? I didn't like the idea. But, I clambered up on the ledge. I moved along very slowly, very cautiously. Once I pressed my body so hard against the tunnel wall I almost pushed myself off the ledge.

The ledge was kind of slimy, too, and twice I almost slipped off.

I breathed a deep sigh of relief when I reached the outside and daylight. The ledge curved right on around the exit so I didn't have to get wet reaching the land.

Along the outside of the tunnel there were structures built like telephone booths, except they were all closed in. I opened the first one I came to. I looked in and jumped back. On the floor was a head with no body attached to it. Once my heart stopped acting like a trip-hammer, I took a closer look. It was part of another exhibit. Those dioramas are changed every summer, and the materials for the changes, costumes, bodies and so on are stored in these cubicles.

I walked on down the side of the tunnel until I came to a spot where I could hear Oscar's barking loud and clear. It was right behind another cubicle. Only this one was locked. I raced back to the tunnel's edge, and hurried as fast as I could along that slippery ledge back to Brains, the boat and Oscar.

"There's a padlock on the door right behind this exhibit," I told Brains. "It's the only one with a padlock on it. All the others haven't any locks. And the padlock on this one is new." Boy, was I ever excited at my discovery.

"We'll have to see if we can get in from this side then, Operative Three. There must be an opening."

Brains climbed out of the boat onto the ledge. Oscar was still barking. I was afraid someone would hear him and investigate.

"We'll have to work fast," Brains said. "Since we can't shut Oscar up." Brains was worrying about the same thing I was. Someone might hear the seal.

Oscar hindered us in another way, too. Brains and I had clambered from the ledge up into the scene itself. I found myself stepping on John Smith's face. Brains bumped into the upraised hatchet. We inspected the background carefully for any kind of opening.

At first—nothing. Finally I spotted a line that could mark a door. But Oscar was standing as firm as a palace guard in front of it.

"Sorry, Oscar, mine friend," I said. "This will hurt me more than it will hurt you." So saying, I gave the seal one fast slap on his rump. Oscar slithered to the front of the scene, gave one affronted bark and kerplopped into the water.

The door, we discovered, was a very narrow one. Painted like the stage set, it was camouflaged from the tunnel sightseers. Thank heaven, it opened easily.

As we eased it open, we heard a groan. It was too dark to see.

"Is that you, Professor?" Brains asked.

We got a grunt for our answer. Brains and I dropped to our hands and knees. By feeling our way, we found

a man bound hand and foot and gagged. I felt the top of the man's head. It was the professor, all right. I could tell by that wild mane of hair of his.

We worked frantically on his bonds and freed him quickly.

"Ach, Mine throat. Mine mouth. Mine hands and feet. And mine back," the professor moaned.

"Can you stand up, Professor?" Brains asked.

"I vill try."

He had a tough time getting up. Brains and I had backed out of the cubicle, back into the diorama, to give him room. We could hear him struggling. He had been in a cramped position for so long it was hard for him to get his tired old bones and muscles to coordinate.

"Hurry, Professor! Hurry!" Brains urged. "Someone might come along any moment."

Oscar was really giving out with the barks now. He was back on the ledge, flapping first one way then another along it but keeping close to all of us.

Finally the professor came through the narrow slit of a door.

"Into the boat. Fast." I said.

The professor didn't ask any questions. He did as I said. Oscar leaped into the boat with him, clapping his flippers and barking for joy.

I took time to stand old Pocahontas back on her feet. Then we hopped into the boat and started backing out.

The tunnel was too narrow to turn the boat around.

Backing out wasn't easy. The stern kept bumping on the sides of the tunnel. I felt it was a race against time, and we were turtles.

We made it, after what seemed like hours. I'd had all of that tunnel I ever wanted. Never again will you get me into one of them, even for fun.

Those amusement park workers must have had a hard night. Oscar's barking hadn't waked any of them up. Could be, too, that the tunnel muffled the sound. Once outside the tunnel, I pointed the boat toward the professor's cottage and gave the motor full throttle. Brains sat up front with the professor, talking to him, but I couldn't hear what they said. The motor made too much noise.

As we neared Knob Point, I cut the motor.

"Want to get the creel now?" I asked Brains.

"Nein! Nein!" the professor answered. "I must to home get for mine animals. Please. You goot boys could come back for the money yet."

That was my answer, so I started up again and we took the professor home.

Brains and I helped him up the path. His joints were still aching, but he wasn't in such bad shape. For an old man he had plenty of comeback power.

"How long were you locked up in that place, Professor?" I asked.

"Time I don't know. It is late in the afternoon—almost dark. I have just fed mine Xenophon. Blackie is there. Then he ties me up again after I am finished eating. He pulls out a big knife." The professor stretched his hands apart to show us the size. It couldn't have been as big as the professor indicated. It would have to have been a sword.

"In mine back he is holding the knife. He tells me we go for little walk. If I try to get away, or shout, into mine back he will push the knife. I am helpless."

The professor halted and leaned against a tree to rest.

"Blackie, he brings me to where you are finding me. He puts a gag in mine mouth and ties mine feet. Then he leaves me. All around me I hear sounds of peoples having goot times. But I can not call out for help. My mouth is bound tight." The professor rubbed his hand against his mouth and then opened and shut it several times.

"And mine poor Xenophon," the professor moaned. "He is gone. Dot Blackie, I could his neck wringing."

"I don't think you have to worry about Xenophon," Brains said. He dug his hand into a pocket and brought out the mouse. I hadn't even seen him take it in the morning.

I can't find the words to tell you how happy the professor was at getting his beloved mouse back. He took the mouse, and cuddled it against his cheek, mur-

muring over and over again, "Ach, mine little Xenophon. Mine Xenny. Mine Xenny."

Now I'm not afraid of mice like girls are, but also I'm not in love with them. With me, a mouse is still a mouse, even if it can dance.

After a few more moments, we continued up to the cottage. Oscar stayed right with us, yapping at the professor's heels.

The professor went immediately into the trailer-zoo. The animals gave him a royal and plenty noisy welcome. Brains and I stayed outside.

"We might as well go for the money, Operative Three," Brains said. "The professor won't even miss us."

"Okay, Operative X. Once we get the money, we're home free."

That's what I said. But that isn't what happened.

Chapter 16

The Battle of Lake Carmine

I felt pretty good, and I know Brains did too. We had rescued the professor, freed him from his kidnappers and now we were on our way to get the money.

"Looks as if the firm of Benton and Carson has done it again, Operative X," I said. We were moving smoothly over the water, aiming for Knob Point.

"To a certain degree, yes, Operative Three," my partner replied. "But we're not in the clear yet—not altogether."

"What could happen now?" I demanded.

"Well, for one thing, we haven't retrieved the money yet. Blackie was convinced we were diving for it. There

164

is nothing to prevent his engaging in a similar operation."

I hadn't thought of that. Blackie had access to skin diving equipment. It could be rented at Wonder Park.

"And even if he hasn't searched the bottom, as we did, we still must get the money and turn it over to the professor," Brains continued.

"But that ought to be easy. You locate the money again with your detector. I dive for it. We speed back to the professor's with it and give it to the old gent."

"You make it sound very simple, Operative Three. Are you forgetting that Blackie must still want to get his hands on that money? Desperately so now. He must know that he will face a kidnapping charge. He will need that money to get out of the country."

I didn't feel quite so good after listening to Brains' calm, well-reasoned opinion. Blackie was still a threat.

"And another thing, Operative Three," Brains went on. "Just whose money is it?"

"Why the professor's, of course," I replied.

"Think back, Operative Three. Don't you remember the professor said that the money wasn't his? I believe I can quote you exactly how he said it: 'Dot money— gone, and not even mine was it.' "

Brains' attempt to imitate the professor's guttural, Germanic accent was a howl. But the thought the statement contained was anything but.

"Whose money could it be, then?" I wanted to know.

"I feel, Operative Three, that there is some connection between the professor and the girl Gretchen. Just what, I am unable to say at this moment. I feel, though, that we shall know soon. I believe the money may be the key."

"You mean she may know whose money it really is?"

"I frankly don't know, Operative Three. I don't want to speculate on the matter until I have more facts in hand."

I wondered where we were going to get more facts. But we were off Knob Point by now, and I started putting on the diving equipment.

Brains had me maneuver the boat for ten minutes before he was certain he was over the spot where we had first found the money.

"If I am right, Operative Three, that creel should be within a ten-foot radius below us."

"So try the detector, anyway. Let's be as sure as we can."

Brains dropped his detecting device overboard. I took an oar and paddled slowly, barely moving the boat. Brains had the headphones on, and his eyes were glued to the indicator dial. He looked up suddenly, a big smile breaking out on his bony face.

"Got it?" I asked excitedly.

Brains nodded his head vigorously. Over I went. Brains had marked the spot well. It didn't take me more than a minute to locate the creel. The end of the detecting lead was resting right on top of it. I picked up the creel and hugged it to my chest. I sat down on the bottom, feeling just wonderful. The water was warm, very clear this morning, and I could look up and see the boat outlined.

I shifted the creel to my left hand and grasped the detector lead with my right. I was going to give it a tug or two to tell Brains I had the creel. But before I could tug, the lead started jerking up and down, fast. At first I didn't get it. Why was Brains signaling me? The lead kept jerking up and down.

Brains was definitely trying to send me a message. I gulped. We must be in trouble again. I surfaced fast.

"Hurry, Jimmy. Hurry!" I knew Brains was excited and we were in danger because he forgot to use my code name.

I tossed the creel into the boat and clambered over the side.

"What's the trouble? What's happened?"

"Start the motor. I'll hoist the anchor." Brains hadn't answered my questions, but I knew better than to press him for answers now. We were being threatened, even if I didn't know from what direction.

Once we were under way, Brains sat on the center seat, looking aft. I gave the outboard all she would take and headed for the professor's dock.

"While you were on the bottom," Brains shouted at me over the noise of the motor, "I kept a careful lookout. I was looking west, toward the park. I saw a flash of bright light, the sun reflecting off a glassy surface. The flash came from a boat, about a mile away. That's why I started signaling you."

"Blackie?" I shouted my question back, and my spine bones tingled as if they were being played like a xylophone.

"Yes! And his pal! Look!" he pointed back.

I swung around. Sure enough, here came that speedboat again, shooting over the water at full speed. It was throwing up a high wake. And it was headed right for us, closing with us rapidly.

"If Blackie had binoculars, he could have seen me toss the creel in the boat, couldn't he?" I asked.

"I'm afraid so, Operative Three," Brains answered worriedly. "He must know, too, that the professor has been freed. He'll guess that it was us who did it, and that the only reason we'd be out here on the lake is to recover the creel. This is his last chance to get the money. He'll be desperate. He'll try anything!"

We had about a half mile to cover before reaching the professor's cottage. We couldn't possibly make it before being overtaken.

That speedboat could make thirty-five miles per hour. Our boat could do about fifteen.

I thought fast. It would be better to take our chances on land than on the water. Blackie could ram and sink us with no trouble at all. Desperately I yanked on the steering bar and headed for shore.

Blackie saw my maneuver and acted to cut me off. He swerved the speedboat and headed for a point between our boat and the beach.

I waited until he was directly between the shore and us, then cut back to the right sharply. The speedboat was faster, but we could maneuver more rapidly. He couldn't make as tight a turn as we could.

Blackie was desperate, too. He cut to the right, the speedboat heeling over at an angle that made me think he was going to swamp her. And I was hoping he was. But he didn't. He came at us now and it looked like curtains for us.

The speedboat bore down on us like an angry shark. I could see the bottom of the bow, raised out of the water by the boat's terrific speed. Only fifteen feet separated us. We were goners. That boat would strike us and leap right on over as we went to the bottom.

I felt Brains snatch the steering bar. He gave it a yank. Our boat swung around just in time. The speedboat grazed our side with a jarring slam. Suddenly, we were headed in opposite directions. Blackie's boat roared toward the middle of the lake. We were headed shoreward once again.

Blackie put his boat in a wide sweeping turn, heeling way over again. Brains kept us headed for shore. We weren't more than two hundred feet away now. Would we make it? Could Blackie close in fast enough to stop our landing?

He could. He shot past us, swerved, and came at us again. Brains was maneuvering our boat in a zigzag pattern. We were like a freighter trying to dodge a submarine.

This time, Blackie nearly got us. He struck our bow and sent us into a dizzy spin. Brains and I nearly went overboard from the impact.

Brains regained control of our boat. I looked up. The professor's dock was only a hundred feet away.

"Make for the dock!" I shouted at Brains. "Keep close to shore."

Brains was bent forward. His face was grim. The back of his hand was white, he was gripping the steering bar so tightly.

We were only thirty feet from the dock when Blackie hit us again. This time we really got it. He rammed into us just behind our bow. The speedboat plowed right on over us. I was flung out over the stern of our boat. Brains plunged over the starboard side.

I gasped, fighting for breath in the roiled water. Suddenly I heard a crash. I shook my head and wiped the water from my eyes. Blackie had hit us so close to shore that he didn't have enough water left to maneuver in. He had smacked onto the beach. He and his confederate had been pitched out. I could see them, lying on the beach, stunned.

I was standing in about four feet of water. Don't ask me how it happened, but I found myself with the creel slung around my neck.

Brains splashed over to my side. We saw our boat spin up on the bank. The motor roared with the prop out of water, then cut out with a puff of steam.

"Let's get out of here. Before they come to," Brains shouted.

The water held us back as we slogged toward the shore by the dock. The more effort we made, the more the water seemed to slow us up. We reached the dock. I looked over my shoulder.

Blackie and his accomplice were on their feet, coming at us at a dead run.

Chapter 17

Something Fishy

Brains and I started running up the path toward the cottage. We had a lead of about twenty-five feet on Blackie and his pal. We kept ahead of them until the creel hanging around my neck and swinging crazily from side to side smacked Brains on the side of the head and sent him sprawling. I stopped. Brains leaped back to his feet. Blackie was only a few feet behind us now.

I spotted a small path leading off the main one. I grabbed Brains by the arm and yanked him onto it. The path was narrow, winding with bramble bushes pressing in on each side. My arms became streaked with red scratches. Brains was taking it, too.

I didn't know where this path led, and I didn't care. Anywhere away from Blackie was all right with me. Only Blackie stayed right behind us. The path started curving around, back toward the main path. All it did, it turned out, was to run in a half circle leading away from the main path only to curve right back to it.

Both of us exploded out of the small path onto the main one. Standing there waiting for us was Blackie's accomplice. He was between us and the cottage.

"Stop 'em, Kenny," we heard Blackie call out. "I'm coming up."

We were trapped. If we headed back to the beach, Blackie and Kenny could pin us down by the water. We couldn't get past Kenny. He was a big guy and plenty mean-looking. We retreated back down the path about fifteen feet. There just wasn't any other way for us to go, water or no water.

I put my hand down to steady the swinging creel and the lid must have been open because my hand went inside it. Ugggh! My hand plunged into a messy, slimy bunch of herring. Those fish of Oscar's, submerged for over two days, had become sodden and mushy. They had also become slippery. That gave me an idea. And not a moment too soon, either.

Blackie popped back on to the main path. He and Kenny stood there together for a moment, panting, then they started toward us. That's when I went into action.

"Head for the lake, Brains," I called. Brains didn't question my order. He moved.

I came right behind him. I moved a little slower, because about every four feet, I dropped a slippery herring. I littered that path with dozens of the smelly, but very slippery fish.

"Run for it, Brains," I shouted. Brains took off like a rocket. I was right behind him. Blackie and Kenny raised a shout and started to chase us.

I must have been inspired when I dropped those fish. Blackie didn't miss a one. One foot hit the first fish. He lost his balance. Regaining it, his other foot hit the second one. He recovered slightly and came on again. Ke-plunk! He hit my next fish booby trap and took a header! He landed face down right on the spot where I had emptied the remainder of the herring. Kenny, unable to check himself, plunged over Blackie and the two of them sprawled on the path.

Blackie pushed Kenny off and sat up with a howl of rage. His hands clawed at his face. It was full of dead, smelly pieces of fish.

The scene was just like an old-time comedy on TV. But neither Brains nor I were in a position to laugh. Just then, we saw another sight, a beautiful one. Down the path, running hard, came the most welcome sight in the world, Officer McKeon. Behind him, puffing away, came the professor.

McKeon halted over the fallen Blackie and Kenny.

"Stay right where you are," he ordered. His voice had all the power and command a police officer could muster. "Don't try to get up, or I'll let you have it," he said. He towered over the two men. Officer McKeon is big and broad with muscles on his muscles.

Blackie looked up through fish-smeared eyes. He didn't move. He knew when he was licked.

"Hello there, Jimmy. Hiya, Brains. Looks like the marines got here just in time." There was a big, happy grin on Officer McKeon's face.

"You must have gotten my note," Brains said.

I was wondering how Officer McKeon happened to be on the spot at the right moment. Brains' mention of his note made me remember.

"It must be eleven o'clock," I said foolishly.

"Ten after, Jimmy," McKeon said, glancing at his wrist watch. "Why? Brains told me to meet you here at eleven. What I don't understand, though, is how you boys managed to time it so well. I mean, enticing these two crooks to this cottage just in time for me to nab them."

"I guess there must be a lot of things you don't understand yet, Officer McKeon," I said. "Lots of things I still don't understand."

"Well, I believe I know most of what's been going on," McKeon said. "The professor put me pretty well in the picture. One or two details I'll need from you two. One thing I already know. Blackie and his friend are in for a long stay as guests of the government—prison guests, that is."

We were all so interested in what we were saying that none of us heard another boat that had pulled up during our conversation. I nearly jumped out of my still-wet skin when a voice behind us shouted sternly:

"Now don't move. Any of you."

What now? I thought. More confederates of Blackie's? Were we going to lose out just when it seemed we had won?

We all swung around to see two men come striding up the path.

"We saw the whole thing," the man in the lead said. "We saw you crazy kids and that speedboat playing touch football."

Oh, brother, what was this man saying!

"We're members of the Lake Carmine Volunteer Boat Patrol. There's been entirely too much outboard and speedboat hot rodding recently. Dangerous to other boaters and to swimmers. You're going to come along with us. We'll see that none of you get to use a boat for the rest of the summer."

The man stepped forward. He meant business.

"This is the livin' end," I thought. "Beached for the whole vacation—maybe for my whole life!"

"Just a moment, sir." Officer McKeon stepped over Blackie and Kenny.

"I think I can give a satisfactory answer to what you have just witnessed. I'm Officer McKeon of the Crestwood Police Department. These boys are my friends. I can vouch for them. They weren't indulging in any foolish boat hot rodding. They were risking their lives to protect and help this gentleman here." He pointed to the professor.

In another couple of minutes, Officer McKeon filled the men in. Their angry stares at Brains and me turned to expressions of amazement and admiration as they listened to our good policeman friend.

"But I am mighty glad you came along when you did," Officer McKeon said. "I'll need help in taking these men to the proper authorities. I actually have no jurisdiction here at Carmine. Although, of course, a policeman is always on duty no matter where he is."

"We'll be glad to do anything we can. Tell us how we can help," the patrol leader said.

"Could you take me and these prisoners down to Wonder Park? Your boat large enough?"

"Sure. Plenty large. And we'll be happy to help you escort them."

"There's a State Police telephone box at the park. This is a job for the State from here on in . . . All right, you two, on your feet." Officer McKeon nudged Blackie with the toe of his shoe. Blackie and his pal got up.

"No tricks now. Just march right down that path and into the boat."

Blackie and Kenny marched. McKeon and the two boat patrolmen followed. Brains, the professor and I brought up the rear.

"See you boys in an hour or two," McKeon called as the boat shoved off. "Talk about your busman's holiday. Here I come out to the lake for some skin diving, and I'm a policeman again."

I knew he wasn't really complaining. Officer McKeon's too good a cop for that. Anyway, he was smiling.

"And I'll see you again, too," Blackie shouted angrily at the professor. "You old buzzard! I'll get back at you if it's the last thing I do."

The professor remained silent.

"And that girl—she just wants that money. She doesn't want any part of you. You'll find that out."

The professor looked sad.

"She was in on this with me."

"Ach, nein! Nein. It couldn't be. Neffer!" The professor moaned.

"Oh, yeah! That's what you think. Ask them kids—I'll bet they seen me with her plenty in the last coupla days."

The professor looked at us. I turned my head away. So did Brains. From what we had overheard, Blackie could well be right.

"All right. That's enough. You keep your mouth closed," Officer McKeon said. The boat pulled away and headed down-lake for Wonder Park.

The professor looked at us sadly. "So much you two goot boys have done for the old professor. Maybe you could do me one more thing?"

"Sure, Professor. Anything." Brains and I answered together.

"You could maybe to a camp called Sandy Cove taking me?"

Of all the requests the professor could have made, that was the one I least wanted to fulfill. I didn't want to be around when the professor met Gretchen, even though I was curious.

"Okay, Professor," I said. "If the boat is still working."

As I walked over to it, I hoped the boat was out of commission.

Chapter 18

"Grossvater!"

Our boat hadn't taken as much of a beating as I expected. The port gunwale, just behind the bow, was stove in. That's where it had been struck by the bow of Blackie's boat. The crack didn't extend clear down to the water line, so the boat shouldn't take on much water.

It was the motor I was most worried about. It had raced at run-away speed for a few seconds when the prop was kicked out of the water as the boat ran aground.

Brains and I tugged the boat back into the lake. We climbed in. The boat wasn't leaking too much. Next I tried the motor. It didn't start at the first pull, nor the second or third. On the fourth try she caught, sputtered through the first firings, then started purring smoothly.

"Okay, Professor. She's all right," I called. "Hop in."

The ride across the lake to Sandy Cove was grim. The professor sat with his head bowed. I could see his lips moving, his head shaking from side to side. I didn't say anything and neither did my partner Brains. What was there to say? I just steered. Brains bailed the boat when it needed it.

I put the bow of our boat gently on the beach right alongside the camp's dock. A short distance away a swimming class was in progress. I didn't see Gretchen at first. She was with the swimmers, but she was wearing a bright red bathing cap, so I couldn't see that bright, sun-streaked hair of hers.

She saw us. She shooed her flock ashore, waved in our direction, then came toward us running lightly and gracefully. Brains, the professor and I were standing on the beach by the boat.

"Gramps! Gramps!" I heard Gretchen call.

The next moment she threw her wet arms around his neck. The professor held her in his bear-like arms and lifted her off her feet in a great big hug.

"Mein Liebchen! Mein Liebchen! Mein kleines Maedchen!" the professor said happily. Tears were running down his cheeks.

"Ach, Grossvater! Grandfather!" Gretchen cried back. Her blue eyes were tear-filled too.

"What are they saying, Brains?" I asked.

"My knowledge of German is mostly limited to scientific words. However, I do know that 'liebchen' means sweetheart. And 'maedchen' is girl. 'Kleines,' of course, is 'little.' "

"And I can figure out 'grossvater.' Means grandfather, doesn't it?"

Brains nodded his head.

The reunion between "grossvater" and granddaughter went on for several minutes and got happier and tearier by the minute. For a girl who had been conniving with some rats against a nice old man, she was putting on a good show. This act, I thought, was the cruelest thing she had ever done to the professor. If he had seen Gretchen with Blackie and overheard their conversations, he'd be crying in a different way. Should Brains and I tell him?

After a while the hugging and crying and reunioning and German-talking let up a bit. The professor turned to us.

"Ach, Gretchen, these two goot boys you should be knowing. They my life have saved."

Before we could introduce ourselves, the professor went into a long string of German words. I couldn't understand any of what he was saying. I figured he was telling Gretchen about how he had been kidnapped by Blackie and how we had saved him.

"And not only me are they saving, they are saving your money, too."

I looked at Brains. "The money is *Gretchen's?*" he asked, hoarsely.

"Ja. The money I am saving for many years for Gretchen to finish her schooling. I am wanting her to go to college."

"So that's what you meant, Professor," Brains said, "when you said the money wasn't yours."

"Ja. Yes. Soon as I save money and put it in the creel, then it no longer belongs to me. It is for meine Enkelin— dot means 'granddaughter.' I save long time to get enough."

There was a pause and we told Gretchen our names. I don't think the professor ever did know us by anything other than "mine goot boys."

"Why I must know your sister, Jimmy," Gretchen said to me. "There's a counselor at the camp across the cove named Ann Carson. Is she your sister?"

"Yes, she is," I replied in a surly voice. She wasn't going to pull that baby-blue-eyed doll stuff on *me*.

I glanced at Brains. He nodded his head at me as if to say, "Go ahead, spit it out." So I did. "Miss Rand," I said very formally, "why were you palling around with that rat Blackie?"

From then on things went easier. Explanations came thick and fast. Two summers before, Gretchen had visited the professor and travelled with his show for a few weeks. That was the first year Blackie had gone to work for the professor. So, Blackie knew Gretchen, and Gretchen knew Blackie.

"You just misunderstood our conversation, Jimmy," she said to me. "Of course I was worried about my grandfather. I knew he was coming to the lake, although I didn't know exactly when. And then one day, I was taking a hike through the woods with a group of my girls, and we came upon the trailer-zoo. I knew it was grandfather's, but I couldn't understand where he had gone. I knew he would never abandon his animals. I went back in the evening to look for him."

"Then that Blackie, he sees mine Gretchen. He is very worried she will find out everything is not what it seems like," the professor cut in.

"Blackie told me that Grandfather had taken the bus to Middlebury to see an old circus friend, Chick Corelli," Gretchen went on.

"Ah, yes," Brains said. "We've been wondering who 'Chick' was."

"Then Blackie and I talked over old times, chatting like a couple of old friends. And to think that, all the time, he had poor Grandfather tied up. . ." She put her arm around his shoulders.

"Did you happen to chat about the money your grandfather was saving to give to you?" I asked. I was recalling the remark Blackie had made about dollars.

"Yes," Gretchen replied. "As a matter of fact, it was Blackie who brought it up. He asked me several times how much I thought I was going to get. He sounded so friendly, so genuinely interested."

"He was interested, all right." I said.

Everything was becoming as clear as the water in Sandy Cove. Blackie's shouting that Gretchen was just after the professor's money had sounded bad to us. Now we knew he had just been trying to hurt the professor.

We knew also that if we hadn't known Blackie was a baddie we wouldn't have been so suspicious of Gretchen's conversations with him. Actually, her words were completely innocent. It was just that they sounded suspicious due to the circumstances.

"You have saying here in this country—all is goot that is ending up goot."

"Yes, Professor," Brains replied. "All's well that ends well." He tried to smile, but to Brains, a cliché is a cliché.

A bell rang out from the woods near the camp buildings.

"That's dinner," Gretchen said. "I've got to take care of my kids."

"Do you want us to take the professor back with us?" I asked.

"Oh, no. He can have dinner with us. Then I'll take

him back. Would you both like to stay, too?"

"Thank you, Gretchen," I said, "but my mom and dad are expecting us home for lunch."

"You boys come visit me and mine Xenophon and Oscar," the professor said.

"We sure will, Professor," Brains and I replied.

We watched them walk toward the camp buildings. Then we got into our boat and headed for home.

"Now, Operative X," I said to Brains, "we can forget about our code names. We can forget about being detectives and spend the rest of our vacation having a vacation."

Brains frowned as he looked at me.

"A detective can never relax. He must always be on the alert for crime. The firm of Benton and Carson must remain ever vigilant."

"Oh, sure," I replied. "But for the next ten days, why don't we just let Xenophon and Oscar run the firm?"

Brains withered me with a scorching look. "Go jump in a lake," he said.

So I did.